Amy's Missing

Roland Smith

YOUTH SLEUTHS
YS PRESS

Cover Illustration © Michael Roydon 1996
Book Design by Kim Minten

Smith, Roland, 1951-
    Amy's missing / Roland Smith
    p. cm.
    Summary: A teenaged boy and his handicapped neighbor solve the case of a missing little girl.
    LCCN: 96-90096.
    ISBN 0-9651052-0-2

    I. Title.
PZ7.S65766Am 1996   [Fic]
                             QBI96-20162

Acknowledgments

There are a lot of people to thank for making this book possible. Among them...

Zach Teters, Pat Washington, Niki, Shawn & Bethany Krielkamp, Mike Roydon, Brenda Scrivens, Roberta McKay, Jeri Petzel, Kim Minten, Melanie Gill, Stephanie Mazzara, Kristen Behrens, Paul Smailes, Kim Willson-St. Clair, Barbara Kouts, Melissa Otis, Kathleen Squires, Hunter Clarke, the wonderful students at Markham Elementary & Wilsonville Primary, and last but not least my lovely wife, partner, and friend, Marie. If it weren't for Marie you wouldn't be reading this book.

1

Theodore

A pigskin led me to Theodore.

Some friends were over and we were playing football in my backyard. As always, the game was full contact without pads and helmets. My goal for the summer was to stay out of the hospital so I could try out for the Grant High freshman football team in the fall. On the day I met Theodore, this goal didn't look so good.

One of my friends had invited his *big* brother and a few of his brother's *big* friends over to give us some football tips. It was brutal. Especially for me, since I was the one carrying the ball most of the time.

"Okay, Pete," Stanley said. "Here's what we'll do. Run straight out, fake left, then angle right. I'll throw the pigskin right into your bread basket. On three—"

"Wait a second," I complained, desperately trying to pick the clump of grass out of my ear. "We just ran that play and it didn't work."

1

"I know," he said. "It's called strategy, Pete. They won't be expecting it again."

"Why don't we try a quarterback sneak or something," I suggested, noticing that Stanley didn't have a single grass stain anywhere on his body.

"Are you kidding?" Stanley asked. "They'd never fall for it!"

I looked at my other teammates for support, but I didn't find any because Stanley's play meant they wouldn't have to touch the ball, which was fine with them.

"This will work," Stanley insisted, confidently.

It didn't work. I ran straight out, faked left, angled right and collided with a brick wall named, Chris "The Cruncher" Jones.

Cruncher looked down at me and grinned. He was missing a front tooth—very attractive. "The ball went into your neighbor's yard," he said. "Go get it."

I stood up slowly and saw Stanley and my other teammates cowering on the far side of the yard.

"How did you manage to throw the ball over a fifteen foot hedge?" I shouted at Stanley.

"You were down! I had to throw it away. *Strategy*, Pete. I think they're getting tired. Hurry up and get the ball before they recover."

I shook my head in disgust and limped next door.

New neighbors had moved in a couple weeks earlier. I hadn't met them yet and I hoped they didn't mind me going into their backyard without asking. I opened the gate and started poking around in the bushes for the football.

"'You looking for this?"

Startled, I turned around. Across the yard, a kid about my age tossed the football up in the air and caught it. He was in a wheelchair, and by the looks of his thin legs, he wasn't ever going to get out of it.

"I didn't see you," I said, trying to act natural as if he didn't have a handicap.

He threw the football up in the air again.

"We're playing a little football next door," I explained.

"I know. I've been listening to you."

"I hope we didn't disturb—"

He threw the football in a perfect spiral that stung my hands when I caught it. I was amazed. I tossed it back to him and he caught it easily.

"My name's Pete Sanford. We're neighbors."

"Theodore McGee," he said.

"You have a pretty good arm."

"Thanks."

"Hey Pete!" Stanley yelled from the other side of the hedge. "We don't have all day."

"I guess I'd better be going," I said.

Theodore nodded and threw the ball back to me. I started toward the gate, then stopped. It seemed sort of rude to just leave him sitting there. "Do you want to come over?" I asked.

"I don't think so," Theodore said. "Maybe some other time."

"Sure." I opened the gate.

"Wait a second," he said.

I stopped again.

"I wouldn't mind having you come over here sometime," he offered. "If you want."

"Okay," I said, but I wasn't thrilled about the idea.

"Good," Theodore said. "We'll see you around then."

I closed the gate and returned to my own backyard.

"What took you so long?" Stanley demanded.

"Nothing." I threw the ball to him, then looked at the hedge. "Why don't we go over to the park and play?"

"Why?" Stanley asked.

"More room," I said, but this wasn't the real reason.

The truth was that I felt uncomfortable with Theodore sitting in his backyard listening to us doing something that he couldn't do.

2

It's Just The Legs

It took me several days to get back over to Theodore's. I had never been around a disabled person and I was nervous about it. What were we going to talk about? I made the mistake of telling my parents about meeting Theodore. Now, every time I saw them they asked if I had been over to see him. I kept coming up with lame excuses. On the fourth day I even voluntarily pulled weeds and mowed the lawn rather than visit him.

"That's it!" I told myself as I pushed our rickety lawnmower back into the garage. "The next thing I know I'll be cleaning my bedroom and scrubbing the toilet." Before I changed my mind again I ran over to Theodore's and knocked on his front door. His mom opened it with a pleasant smile.

"I'm Pete from next door. Is Theo here?"

"Well, I'm glad to meet you, Pete," she said. "Please come in. Theodore's downstairs."

She led me through the kitchen and opened a door. I expected to see a set of stairs leading down to the basement, but it looked more like a small empty closet.

"It's a lift," she said. "Go ahead. And by the way, he doesn't like to be called Theo or Ted."

"Thanks for the warning," I said and stepped inside.

"Just push the button."

The floor jerked and I started down, ending up in a large daylight basement. I stepped out of the lift, but saw no sign of Theodore.

The basement walls were lined with books all the way up to the ceiling. Aside from playing sports, reading was my favorite activity. I scanned the titles wondering if they all belonged to Theodore. And if the books were his, how did he reach the ones on the upper shelves? Most of the books were paperback novels, but a few of them were huge hardbacks with names like, *Inside the Criminal Mind* and *Homicide Investigative Procedures*. I doubted that those belonged to Theodore and wondered if his dad was a cop.

"You like to read?"

I nearly jumped out of my skin.

"Wheels don't make much noise on carpet," he said, without apology.

His comment made me squirm a little. I stared through the patio door so I wouldn't have to look at his thin, misshapen legs. I felt him glaring at me.

"You see something interesting out there?" he asked, angrily.

"Well, no I—"

"Look," he said, wheeling between me and the door. "I don't give people very long to get used to the fact that I'm glued to this chair. You're embarrassed, but it doesn't embarrass me."

"I'm not embarrassed," I insisted.

"Really?"

"Well," I stammered. "Maybe a little bit."

He grinned. "At least you're half honest. Come on outside, I want to show you something."

I followed him to the patio door. It slid open automatically and he rolled through, then wheeled up to a picnic table. He motioned for me to sit down across from him.

"Okay," he said. "What do you see?"

I looked at him. "I don't understand."

"What do you see?" he repeated.

"You?"

"Very good!" he said, sarcastically. "What do I look like?"

I had no idea where he was going with this. He had unkempt red hair, thick glasses, brown eyes, and pale skin with a lot of freckles. "You look like a kid," I said.

"A normal kid?"

"Yeah, pretty much."

"It's because you can't see the wheelchair."

Now I understood what he was trying to prove. With the chair hidden behind the table he looked like any of my other friends. "You're right," I told him.

"It will take you awhile to get used to the chair," he said. "Imagine how long it took me. You want to arm wrestle?"

"What?" He had to be kidding.

"Arm wrestle," he repeated, putting his elbow on the table.

"I don't think that's a good idea," I stammered. "I mean I've been working out and you—"

"Are you afraid I'll win?"

"No."

"Then let's go."

"Theodore, I'm not going to take it easy on you."

He laughed. "Give it your best shot, neighbor."

I locked hands with him and it was over almost before it began. I'm big for my age and pretty strong. I stared at him. No one had ever beaten me in arm wrestling.

"I thought you weren't going to take it easy on me?"

"I wasn't taking it easy!" And I was telling the truth.

I tried twice more with my right hand and three times with my left. The results were the same. I lost.

"It's just the legs that don't work."

I rubbed my sore wrists. He was right. Everything else on him seemed to be working just fine, in fact, better than fine.

"So, what happened to your legs?" I asked.

"Car accident. When I was a kid."

"I'm sorry."

"I've learned that it isn't the end of the world. Let's go back inside."

We found a plate of sandwiches sitting in the lift and wolfed them down as we talked.

Instead of going to school, Theodore had a tutor who came to his house three times a week.

"It's a lot less hassle," he said. "I'll be graduating from high school next year."

"How old are you?"

"Fifteen."

"A year older than me," I said in amazement. "Maybe I should get a tutor."

"It has its advantages," he agreed.

A phone rang. Theodore reached down and pulled a cordless phone from a holster attached to his chair. "Hello? Yeah...sure. What's the license number?" He took a small notebook out of his shirt pocket and wrote something in it. "And the make?"

He sounded like a used car salesman.

"Uh huh...yeah. It will take awhile. Yeah, okay. Bye."

He slipped the phone back into the holster. "I hate to cut this short," he said. "But something's come up."

I wanted to ask him what it was, but I decided against it. I figured he'd tell me if he wanted me to know. "That's okay," I said. But I was disappointed—I was actually beginning to relax and enjoy myself.

"Do you want to come back?" he asked.

"Sure."

"How about tomorrow?"

"Okay."

"In the meantime," he said. "Do you want to borrow a couple of books?"

"Are all these yours?"

"Most of them," he said. "I like mysteries. Detective fiction, things like that. Have you ever read any Chandler or Hammett?"

"I don't think so," I said, knowing full well I hadn't. The only mysteries I'd read were The Hardy Boys—all fifty-eight of them. After that mystery marathon I decided to stay away from mysteries for awhile.

"Good," he said as he pulled a couple of paperbacks off the shelf and handed them to me. One was called, *The Big Sleep* by Raymond Chandler. The other was called, *The Continental Op* by Dashiell Hammett.

"Hope you like them," Theodore said. "I'll see you tomorrow."

3

Private Eyes

As soon as I got home I cracked open *The Continental Op* and started reading. The book was a series of short stories about Operatives (called Op's for short) working for the Continental Detective Agency in San Francisco. The stories were great. I finished the book before I went to sleep that night.

The next morning I started reading *The Big Sleep* by Raymond Chandler. Before I knew it, the morning was gone. It was about a private eye named, Philip Marlowe solving a case in Los Angeles and it was even better than the first book.

Both books were written in the 1930's and reminded me of the old black and white movies my parents liked to watch on TV. I never paid much attention to these movies because I like science fiction and action pictures, but after reading the books I decided to catch a couple of these black and white films to see what they were about.

During the next week I went over to Theodore's almost every day. He gave me more mysteries to read, which were just as good as the first two. Theodore seemed to know a lot about everything, but he didn't act like a know-it-all. He was a good listener, had a great sense of humor, and overall, he was very easy to be around.

My parents were very happy about the whole thing. Especially my mom. She thought there was no way I could possibly get in trouble with a friend confined to a wheelchair. She didn't know Theodore. And it turned out that I didn't know him very well either.

Theodore's cordless phone was constantly ringing. In fact, he got more phone calls than my older sister Teri did, which was hard to believe. When the phone rang he snapped it from the holster like a gunslinger pulling out his six shooter. Sometimes he would just mumble a "yeah" or "okay," then hang up and continue talking with me as if nothing had happened. Other times the phone conversations where longer and more involved, but I still couldn't get a sense of who he was talking to, or what he was talking about. He'd say words like, SS number, data, records, credit card, password, then jot things down in his notebook. It didn't make any sense and when I asked him who was calling, he'd tell me it wasn't important and quickly change the subject.

A couple of times when the phone rang, Theodore actually excused himself and went into the other room to talk. And this was another mystery I couldn't figure out. Was he hiding something? Or was he just trying to act mysterious to impress me?

He had never shown me the other basement room, which I assumed was his bedroom. The door was always closed. At first I thought he just didn't want me in there because it was messy or something—like that would bother me. But I soon realized it was more than this. He not only didn't want me in the room, he didn't want me to *see* in the room. He had a way of getting through the door so quickly that I couldn't peek inside—not an easy maneuver in a wheelchair.

The third time Theodore went into the room, he was gone a long time. After waiting about twenty minutes I began to wonder how Philip Marlowe would handle this situation. He'd probably kick the door in, grab the phone from Theodore, and phone-whip him with it. But this wasn't a black and white movie and I wasn't Philip Marlowe, so I decided the best way to handle the situation was to go home.

I was halfway across the backyard when Theodore called out.

"Hey, Pete! Where are you going?"

"I have some things to do," I said, sharply.

Theodore looked thoughtful, then said, "I'm sorry that took so long."

I didn't say anything.

"You're probably wondering what's going on," he continued.

"It's none of my business," I told him.

"Why don't you come back inside. I have something to show you."

"That's what you said when you beat me at arm wrestling," I reminded him.

Theodore grinned. "Well, this is a little different."

He was wrong. It wasn't a little different it was *a lot* different. I followed him back inside and he opened the secret door. My eyes almost popped out of my head. The room was filled with phones, fax machines, computers, and other electronic gear I had never seen before. All the computers were on and groups of numbers were flashing across the screens.

"You're a computer hacker!"

"Not exactly," he said with a nervous laugh.

"Then why do you have all this equipment?"

"Are you interested in computers?"

"Yeah," I answered. "We have an old clunky computer at home, but nothing like this. I've wanted to get a new one, but we can't afford it. But that doesn't answer my question, Theodore. What are you doing with all this stuff?"

He motioned me to an empty chair and I sat down. There was a hospital bed on the far side of the room. Hanging above it were a series of stainless steel bars, which he must use to get in and out of bed. Near the bed, attached to the wall, was an elaborate exercise machine with pulleys and weights. This explained how he had destroyed me at arm wrestling.

"I don't know exactly where to start," he began, a little nervously. "I was going to wait a couple of weeks and then talk to you about it." He hesitated. "You know those books I gave you to read?"

I nodded.

"Have you ever thought about being a private detective, or confidential investigator?"

"Not really," I said. Although, I had actually been thinking about it a lot. "Why?"

"Well...," he stammered. "I run a private detective agency."

"What?" I shouted. "You're only fifteen years old!"

15

"Shhhh!" He pointed upstairs.

I lowered my voice. "Are you saying your parents don't know about all this computer stuff? Come on Theodore!"

"Of course they know about it. They just don't know what it's used for. They think I'm interested in computers."

"Interested? You probably have better equipment than the FBI!"

"Not better," he said calmly. "But some of it is just as good."

"Seriously, Theodore," I continued, trying to give him a way out. "What do you do with all this stuff?"

"Seriously, Pete, I'm a Private Investigator, or Private Eye if you like. I've solved a lot of cases in the past two years. In fact, one of the reasons we had to move here was because of the death threats."

"Death threats?" Now I was beginning to understand. His legs weren't his only disability. He'd also gotten banged on the head and there was permanent brain damage. "What death threats?"

"I got someone arrested and they started hassling me and my parents. When I have time I'll tell you the whole story."

I figured the only reason he couldn't tell me the whole story now was because he hadn't made it up yet.

"That's why I don't want anyone to find out about

what I do down here," he continued.

"Didn't the death threats make your parents a little suspicious about what you're doing with this equipment?"

"Absolutely! But they never quite figured out what happened. Like you, they didn't believe that a kid was capable of all this."

"All of what? What is it you do exactly?"

"It's a little hard to explain. I gather and sort information, then analyze it. Everyone in the world leaves a shadow on the information highway. You just have to know where to look and what to look for."

"Your parents must have a lot of money," I said, trying to get him off the subject before he lied his way into a corner he couldn't get out of. "This stuff isn't cheap."

"My parents didn't pay for any of this," he said, obviously hurt. "I paid for it with proceeds from my work."

"Proceeds?"

"Case fees," he explained.

Settlement fees, I thought. He probably got a pile of insurance money after his accident.

"You don't believe me do you?"

"I don't know, Theodore. This is just—"

"Too bad," he interrupted. "I wanted you to be one of my operatives."

Before I could react, the phone rang again. Theodore

snapped it out of the holster before the second ring and started talking. It looked like it was going to be another long conversation. I stood up to leave.

Theodore covered the mouthpiece and said, "I have to take care of this. I'll talk to you later."

"Okay," I said, but he didn't hear me because he was already back on the phone.

4

Uncle Willy

As soon as I got home I went up to my bedroom to think things over.

I wanted to believe Theodore was telling the truth, but I couldn't quite get there. There was no way a kid could own a detective agency. The only explanation for this fantasy was that he had read too many private eye books and somehow this had driven him over the edge. I decided to cut back on my visits to Theodore's and get serious about football again. This didn't last very long.

The next day after practice I found myself staring out the window at his house wondering what he was really doing in the basement with all that electronic equipment. If he wasn't a private eye, what were all the phone calls about?

I went out into our backyard and threw the ratty tennis ball a few times for my Australian cattle-dog,

Spike. On the fourth throw I intentionally tossed the ball over the fence into Theodore's backyard. I walked over, opened the gate, and started looking for the ball in the bushes.

Behind me, I heard the patio door slide open and Theodore rolled outside. I turned around and faced him. "So what does an operative do?"

"Come on in and we'll talk about it," Theodore said as if he had been expecting this question all along. He turned his chair around and I followed him inside.

It seems like Op's did just about everything.

"They gather information, follow people, do surveillance, ask questions, set up telephone taps—"

"Aren't taps illegal?" I asked.

"Only if you get caught," Theodore answered. "That's why you have to be careful."

"What other illegal things do Op's do?"

"Nothing serious. In order to solve cases, rules have to be bent and laws have to be tweaked from time to time. We can do things the police aren't allowed to do."

"But what if you get caught tweaking the law?"

"Have you ever heard of a kid going to prison for trying to catch a crook?"

I had to admit that I hadn't.

"So, are you interested?" he asked.

"I don't know," I said.

"I pay ten bucks an hour plus expenses."

"Ten dollars an—"

"I know it isn't much, but we're just getting started here."

To me, ten dollars an hour was a fortune. "Who's we?"

"I have a partner. Well, sort of a partner, my Uncle Willy."

"What do you mean, sort of?"

"You still don't believe me do you?"

It all seemed too fantastic, but I didn't want to tell him this and hurt his feelings.

"Why don't you go down and talk to Uncle Willy?" Theodore proposed. "You can pick up the package he has waiting for me. Our office is at Union Station."

I told him I'd go, figuring that when I didn't find Uncle Willy it would put an end to Theodore's fantasy detective agency and I could quit thinking about it.

I took the bus down to Union Station, which was in an old train depot on the other side of the river. When I got there I rode an old creaky elevator up to the third floor to look for the mythical Uncle Willy and Theodore's detective agency.

I walked down the long hallway reading the names off the doors. *Dave's Import Export. Smither's Talent Agency*. Then, to my surprise:

William Last
YS Detective Agency
Confidential Investigations
Last But Not Least - Since 1927

Which meant that the fantasy wasn't quite over yet. But 1927? If this was true, Theodore's detective agency was started before his grandparents were born. Not likely.

I knocked on the door and heard a woman call from inside, "The door's open!"

I walked in. The woman sitting behind the reception desk was in her early twenties and looked like she belonged in one of my sister's glamour magazines. I started to feel nervous, which is my usual response in the presence of a pretty woman.

She smiled and I started sweating. Other than a phone, the only thing on her desk was a computer.

"You must be Pete," she said. "I'm Margaret. Willy's expecting you. You can go right in." She pointed to a door to her right marked: *Private*. I walked through the door.

An old man with long, swept back, white hair and a dark tan was resting his feet on a huge desk watching a soap opera on a big screen TV.

"Make yourself comfortable, Pete," he said without looking away from the screen. "With any luck, this thing will be over in a moment."

This couldn't possibly be Theodore's uncle, I thought. He was way too old. The guy had to be at least seventy. He wore a carefully knotted red tie and yellow suspenders over a starched white shirt. Hanging on the hall tree behind him was a blue, double breasted pin-striped suit jacket, a tan trench coat, an old fashioned hat, which I think they used to call a Fedora, and a black cane with an ivory handle. He looked like he had just stepped out of one of my parent's black and white private eye movies. Grampa Philip Marlowe.

The office was sparsely furnished. In front of his desk were two chairs and against one wall was an old, overstuffed sofa. There were no filing cabinets, no computer, no books, and nothing hung on the walls. The only thing on top of the desk was a yellow legal-sized note pad, a telephone, a paper coffee cup, and an ashtray filled with thick, disgusting cigar butts, which accounted for the sour smell that was beginning to make my eyes water.

I waited. Uncle Willy didn't take his eyes off the television. He seemed to be as hypnotized by the soap as my older sister was every afternoon when she got home from school. When the show finally ended he switched it off and turned to me shaking his head.

"Pitiful," he murmured.

I wasn't sure whether he was referring to me or to the soap opera he had just finished watching. He opened one of the desk drawers and pulled out a thick manila envelope and set it on the desk.

"So you're the new Op," he said.

He had to be kidding. "I'm not sure."

He stood up, stretched, then limped around to my side of the desk. The limp was pretty bad, which explained the ivory handled cane. He leaned against the desk with his arms folded across his chest and looked at me for a long time without saying a word, which really gave me the creeps.

When he saw that I was about ready to bolt from the office in terror he continued, "Theodore says that you're the new Op and that means you are whether you believe it or not." He picked up the envelope and handed it to me. "You ought to find this case interesting. Everything I have on it is in here. Tell Theodore to give me a call if he has any questions."

Either Uncle Willy was as crazy as Theodore, or he was just playing along with him. I figured that he must make up cases so Theodore would have something to do. Theodore's parents probably knew all about it. In fact, I wouldn't have been surprised if they paid Uncle Willy to do it.

"You're not really Theodore's uncle are you?"

He gave me that hard stare again, then said, "No, I'm not."

"Then who are you?"

"Just an old detective."

"Have you really been in business since 1927?"

"In a manner of speaking," he said. "I was born in 1927."

"I see."

He looked at his watch. "I have an appointment in about forty-five seconds," he said.

Probably another soap opera, I thought. I stood up and started toward the door.

"Hey," Willy said. I turned around. "Theodore's a good kid. He needs your help."

I nodded and left his office.

So the whole thing was a giant fantasy, but Theodore wasn't alone. Willy was helping him. As I rode the bus home I wondered how Theodore could fall for something like that. He seemed way too smart. But I guess he didn't have much else to do. Aside from me, he didn't have any friends—at least he hadn't mentioned any. He was probably pretty lonely, "glued" to that chair of his, as he put it.

I have to admit when I saw the sign on Uncle Willy's door I thought that maybe, just maybe, there was something to all this. But I was kicking myself now for believing, even for a second, that Theodore was actually a confidential investigator and that I might be an operative and make ten bucks an hour. I was too old to play games like this, but I didn't know how I was going to tell Theodore. If I didn't go along with him, our friendship would probably be over before it really got started. And I really liked Theodore, despite this little glitch in his personality.

When I got back to Theodore's he was waiting for me on the patio with an odd smirk on his face. I gave him the envelope.

"So what did you think of Uncle Willy?" he asked.

"Seemed like a nice guy," I said, vaguely.

"What time did you get there?"

"A little before three."

"Then you caught him watching a soap opera?"

"Yeah."

Theodore laughed. "Old Willy has a real thing for soaps."

"So does my sister."

"Well," he said patting the envelope. "I'd better get to work. We'll start tomorrow morning at eight sharp."

"Start what?"

"The case of course," he said impatiently.

He actually thought there was a real case. I felt sorry for him.

"Eight o'clock is kind of early," I said, trying to come up with a way out of this.

"You're telling me," he continued. "I'll probably be up half the night figuring out what we're going to do. But there's no way around it. Cases don't get solved unless you work on them."

I wanted to tell him that I didn't think I'd be able to help him, but before I could say anything he turned his wheelchair around and rolled through the patio door.

"See you tomorrow morning," he yelled, as the door slid closed behind him.

5

Op-portunity

I tossed and turned all night thinking of different ways to tell Theodore I thought he was out of his mind. By the time the sun came up I was so desperate I actually considered asking my parents what I should do.

I went downstairs and found my parents in the kitchen. They were sitting at the table talking excitedly, which wasn't normal for them.

My parents aren't exactly at their best in the morning. Their usual routine is to sit at the kitchen table and say nothing to each other or to us. They read the newspaper and suck down coffee for about half an hour. By the time they're ready to leave for work they can usually manage a few simple sentences like, "Take out the garbage." Or, "Mow the lawn after school."

But this morning was definitely different. They were both smiling and chattering like birds.

"What's going on?" I asked.

"We won a trip!" my mom exclaimed happily. "I went out to get the newspaper and there was a package sitting on the porch with two first class tickets to San Francisco, hotel accommodations—"

"The whole ball of wax," my father chimed in.

I don't know where he came up with these phrases, but he had hundreds of them.

"It'll be like a second honeymoon," my mother said. "We spent our first honeymoon in San Francisco." She raised her eyebrow at my father.

Oh brother! "How did you win?" I asked, changing the subject.

"I don't know," my mom said. "It must have been one of those contest forms I filled out somewhere." I wasn't surprised that she didn't remember. She was a sweepstakes addict. If she won half the contests she entered every year we'd be billionaires.

I looked at the tickets. "When do you leave?"

"Tonight," my father said. "Right after work. They don't give you much warning, but we can't look a gift horse in the mouth."

"We'll be back Monday evening," my mom said. "You and Teri will have to fend for yourselves for a few days."

Teri was my older sister. She was seventeen and this

would be the best news she had heard all summer.

"I want you to do whatever Teri tells you to do," my father added, which he couldn't possibly mean.

Teri didn't like me very much. She was constantly telling me to do all sorts of things, like; go jump in a lake, or play football on the freeway with my friends during rush hour traffic.

I was happy for my parents and glad they were going to get away for a few days, but none of this would help me deal with Theodore's insanity. I ate a quick bowl of cereal, then went into the backyard to throw the ball for Spike and consider my options.

I could always disappear for the day. There was a chance that by the time I got back, Theodore would have forgotten about the whole thing. I'd heard that insane people have very short attention spans. But Theodore seemed to be pretty focused.

I thought about telling Theodore that I was sick and couldn't leave the house. But if I did this and he or his parents happened to see me leave the house I'd be sunk. And I sure didn't want to be stuck in the house with my sister's friends, who I knew would move in as soon as my parents left on their trip.

I even thought about asking my parents if I could go with them to San Francisco. If I begged them they'd probably let me, but I knew they wouldn't be thrilled about it.

By eight o'clock I still didn't know what I was going to do. I waited a few more minutes hoping that something would come up. Nothing did, so I walked over to Theodore's.

I found him in his computer room. He was so busy he didn't even notice me walk in. I watched as he typed on two different keyboards at the same time. Names, numbers, and people's photographs appeared for a split second on each screen, then disappeared replaced by new information and photos. One of the printers was rattling out a long string of paper. Every once and awhile he checked the paper, then looked back at the screens. His red hair was sticking straight up in the air and the dark bags under his eyes were magnified by his thick glasses. He looked like some kind of mad scientist.

I was just about ready to sneak out and forget the whole thing when the phone rang. As he drew it from the holster, he turned and saw me.

"You're late," he said.

"Yeah, I—"

"Just a second," he interrupted. "I have to get this." He answered the phone. "Oh, that's great. Good. We'll get it then. Okay. Bye." He looked back at the computer screen. "I'll be done here in about five minutes. I'm just double checking some stuff."

I waited and watched while he printed out some more things. He gathered them together and put them into a folder.

"That about does it," he said, wearily.

"What's going on Theodore?"

"Have you done much backpacking?"

"Yeah," I said. "Why?"

"You're going to Montana."

"I'm what?" I shouted.

6

Leg Work

"So I fly to Bozeman, Montana. Take a tour bus to Yellowstone National Park. Hike into the wilderness. Infiltrate a religious cult. Find out if a little girl named Amy is there. And hike back out?"

"That about sums it up," Theodore answered, like he was asking me to go to the mall. "But don't forget about taking a photograph of Amy at the commune. We need concrete proof she's there."

"Oh yeah, the photograph. Right." Theodore was out of his mind. "And how am I supposed to pay for a plane ticket to Montana?"

"It's already taken care of. The ticket's waiting for you at the airport. Your plane leaves at six this evening."

"And where do I stay tonight?"

"You have a reservation at the Holiday Inn near the airport in Bozeman. The tour bus leaves tomorrow morning at seven from the hotel. It goes to Mammoth Hot Springs. That's where you'll find the trail head that leads to the commune. I have it all mapped out for you."

"And what's the commune called again?"

"C-O-D-L," he said. "Children Of Divine Light. It's all in the folder."

"Right, and I'm supposed to saunter up to their homestead in the woods and tell them I want to join up."

"From the information I've gathered," Theodore said. "I don't think they'll turn you away. And because of your age, they won't suspect you of being an undercover cop or reporter. They'll accept you with open arms, and with luck, you should be back by Sunday evening."

"And what am I supposed to tell my parents?" I asked. "I'm going to Yellowstone for the weekend— catch you later."

"Didn't you say your parents were leaving town?"

"Yeah, but—"

"If you get back before they do, I don't see any point in telling them."

"Okay then, what do I tell my sister?"

"Tell her you're spending a couple of nights at a friends or something. From what you've told me about her she'll be happy to get rid of you and have the house to herself."

Well, at least he had that right. Teri didn't care where I was as long as it was out of her sight.

"What about money?" I asked.

Theodore opened a drawer, took out an envelope and gave it to me. "This should be enough to cover incidental expenses. Get receipts for everything and give them to me at the end of the assignment. Willy needs them for taxes."

I opened the envelope. There was at least five hundred dollars in fives, tens, and twenties. I was about to tell him I wasn't going to take the money, and more importantly, I wasn't going to Yellowstone, when a loud buzzer went off in the room.

"Incoming parent!" he said. "It's my mom. Quick, put everything in the bag."

Only Theodore would have an alarm to warn him that his parents were approaching. Without thinking I started helping him stuff the maps, photographs, camera, and other gear into a small backpack. We got it zipped closed just as his mother walked into the computer room.

"Oh, hello Pete!" she said. "I didn't know you were down here."

"I came through the backyard," I said.

"That's nice." She looked affectionately at her crazy offspring. "Are you ready to go Theodore?"

"Just about," he mumbled.

"Well, please hurry. We don't want to be late. I'll be upstairs. Good to see you again Pete."

"You too," I said.

She gave me a nice smile and walked out of the room.

"I have to go," Theodore said. "I've got a doctor's appointment."

I wondered if the appointment was with a psychiatrist. Maybe I should get the shrink's phone number and have a conversation with him about his patient's latest delusion.

"Well...," I hesitated. I didn't know what to say to him. "I guess I'll talk to you when you get back."

"Yeah," he said. "Call me when you get to Bozeman."

"What?"

He started to switch off the computer equipment. "I won't be home 'til late. After my appointment, my mom's making me get my hair cut and go shopping, then we're meeting my dad for dinner. We haven't been out in a long time and I promised her I'd go without complaining. Family day. You know how it is."

"Sure." I knew all about family days, but why did he have to have one today? I needed some time to break it to him gently that I thought he was out of his mind. "Theodore," I stammered. "This is just a game you're—"

"No it's not!" he said, harshly. "But I don't have time to prove to you right now that it isn't. A little girl is missing. Her name is Amy. And there's probably not a chance in a million that she's at the C.O.D.L. commune, but it has to be checked out. That's what detective work is all about—running down leads that usually go nowhere. You don't read about this kind of grunt work in books or see it in films, because it's pretty boring. It's just leg work. I'd go to Montana myself to check out this lead, but it would be a little difficult to get through the woods on these." He slapped his legs, making me wince with guilt.

"Look at it this way," he continued. "You'll be getting paid to go camping for a couple of days. The money will help you buy that computer you want. In fact, if Amy's there and you get her photograph I'll *buy* you the computer as a bonus. You can use the money you earned for software."

It would be interesting trying to explain a new computer to my parents. "I still don't know, Theodore," I said.

"I've got to go." He started rolling towards the door. "I'm sure you'll make the right decision. I've written everything down." He turned his wheelchair around and backed it into the lift. "Oh, one more thing. Don't take any of the information or photos of Amy with you. If she's there and something happens you sure don't want to be caught with them. Any questions?"

"Well—"

"Good luck, Pete," he said and disappeared into the ceiling.

7

Amy's Missing

I spread all the gear Theodore had given me out on my bed: binoculars, pocket-sized camera, and map. Along with all this stuff was a folder that included several photographs, background information on the Children Of Divine Light, and a brief summary of "the case" as Theodore called it.

I remembered hearing something about it on the news awhile back.

A little girl named Amy O'Toole disappeared from her backyard on May 4th at three o'clock in the afternoon. She was wearing blue jeans, white Nike tennis shoes, a red tee-shirt, and a pink jacket.

When Amy's mother Sarah O'Toole discovered that Amy was gone she contacted friends and neighbors and they searched everywhere for her. When they couldn't find her they called the police.

The police believed that Amy was the victim of a

random abduction. Posters with Amy's photograph were widely circulated and aired on local news shows for several weeks. A reward of twenty-thousand dollars was offered for information leading to Amy's whereabouts. No one came forward.

Sarah O'Toole had hired the YS Detective Agency to help find her daughter because she felt the police weren't doing enough.

That was about it. There was no mention about why Theodore thought Amy was at the C.O.D.L. commune.

The whole thing seemed ridiculous to me. I would have bet anything that Theodore didn't like the case that Willy had really given him so he had made up one of his own. Even if YS Detective Agency had been hired to find Amy, there was no way they would turn the case over to a kid. Uncle Willy had probably given Theodore a case along the lines of a missing dog or cat.

Amy's photo smiled up at me from my bed. I turned it over and read the note clipped to the back.

> **Subject's Name: Amy O'Toole.**
> **Age: 4 years. Hair: brown. Eyes: blue.**
> **Weight: Approximately 32 pounds.**

Along with this photo there were a couple other shots of Amy. One was of her making a sand castle at the beach. The other was of Amy playing in her back-yard with a puppy. She looked like a happy kid.

I slipped the identification photo into my shirt pocket, then looked at the newspaper photo of Amy's parents. They were young and looked terribly worried. I felt bad for them. They had to be going nuts over Amy's disappearance.

I called the YS Detective Agency to talk to Uncle Willy. He'd be able to tell me if Theodore was really on this case. Unfortunately, all I got was a recording saying that the office was going to be closed for a few days because Willy was out of town.

Next I called my friend, Shawn, to find out what he was doing. He told me that he was grounded and wanted to know if I wanted to help him clean out his parent's garage over the weekend. Forget it.

Then I called Stanley. He told me he was going camping for the weekend.

"I think my dad's plan is to ditch me in the woods and have a cougar eat me," he said. "You wanna come?"

I told him no. Stanley's dad was a professional wrestler whose ring name was Paul Bunyan. Sometimes he carried an ax or a chain saw into the ring with him, depending on his mood.

Camping with Mr. Bunyan was always interesting,

but not necessarily fun. When he wasn't body slamming opponents in the ring he was practicing wilderness survival techniques. His idea of camping was to take a knife, compass, canteen, and us into the most remote, desolate spot he could find and live off the land for a few days. During these trips I learned a lot about how to stay alive in the woods, but I was always very happy to get back home.

At least once during these outings Mr. Bunyan would ditch us and we would have to find our way back to camp or to the car on our own. He said he always kept an eye on us with a spotting scope so we wouldn't get into any real trouble. As we stumbled through the woods our primary concern was what would happen to us if something happened to Mr. Bunyan. If my parents knew what went on during these camping trips Paul Bunyan would have a real fight on his hands.

I don't know why, but I hadn't told Stanley or Shawn about Theodore—and it wasn't because of Theodore's disability. The fact he couldn't walk wasn't even an issue anymore. I just didn't want to tell them until I had Theodore figured out. And I was a long way from that point.

I went downstairs to make a sandwich. Teri came

into the kitchen as I was stacking a pile of baloney and cheese on a piece of bread.

"Clean up your mess," she snapped.

Instead of saying anything I plopped a huge spoonful of mayonnaise on the pile. Teri hates to be ignored and the sight of mayonnaise and meat usually makes her gag.

"So what are you doing this weekend?" she asked looking away from my gut bomb.

I put a slice of bread on top of the pile and pushed it down so I'd be able to get my mouth around it.

"I asked you a question," she said nastily.

I walked into the living room with my sandwich and flopped onto the sofa and turned on the television with the remote.

Teri followed me and stood in front of the screen. "I asked you a question," she repeated.

"My mowf if full," I said.

"Well, I'm having some people over this weekend and I don't want you or your sicko friends bugging us," she announced.

I pointed the remote at her and pushed the button.

"I mean it Pete!" she screamed. "I don't want you ruining my weekend."

The signal must have passed right through her body

because the TV channel changed. Too bad it didn't change her, I thought.

"I'm going camping," I said as a joke.

"For the weekend?"

I nodded.

"With who?" she asked suspiciously.

"Stanley."

"And mom and dad said it was all right?"

My parents didn't like Stanley. They thought he was out of control. And they were right.

"I haven't asked them," I said.

"Well, there's no way they'll let you go anywhere with *him*."

I shrugged my shoulders and smiled. "Then I guess we'll just have to hang around here," I said.

"Not with Stanley you're not."

"No choice. My house too, Sis. Stanley and I don't have anything to do. Hope your friends like him."

She went pale. When it came to getting on people's nerves nobody could beat Stanley. He'd think nothing about walking into a room full of strangers—on his hands. Or blowing his nose on a the tablecloth in a nice restaurant. I'd seen him do these things more than once.

"Well," she sputtered. "Maybe you *could* go camping with him."

43

"Nah," I said. "mom and dad would never let me."

"Don't tell them," she said, in a panic. "After all, they're going to be gone and I'll be in charge."

"You mean you'd let me go?"

"Is Stanley's father going?"

I nodded. She shuddered with revulsion.

"You'd have to be home before mom and dad got back. And you'd have to promise not to tell them you went. They'd skin me alive."

"What if a cougar mauls me?" I asked.

"Paul Bunyan would have to bring your remains out of the woods and dump them in the backyard. I'd tell mom and dad you ran over yourself with the lawnmower."

Some sister.

Before the run-in with my sister I had no intention of going to Montana, but after I talked to her I wasn't so sure.

I went up to my room and called the airport and asked if they had a ticket waiting for me. They did. One thing I had to say about Theodore, he took his fantasies seriously, and he had a lot of money to feed them.

I started playing with the idea. What was the worst thing that could happen? I'd go to Yellowstone, spend a couple days hiking around, then come home. Maybe there was a cult up in the woods and maybe Amy was there. Why not pretend I was a private eye for a couple of days? After all, it was just leg work.

The more I thought about it, the more I liked the idea. I wondered if Theodore was going to pay me ten bucks an hour while I slept out under the stars. I should have asked him.

8

The Flight

The plan came together perfectly—almost. I took a bus to the airport. I showed the man at the airline counter my student identification and he gave me my ticket. I strolled through the metal detector and ran the backpack through the x-ray machine. On the way to the gate I stopped at a snack stand and bought a couple of candy bars. I walked to my gate and almost bumped into my parents. I thought I was going to have a heart attack.

I ducked behind a big pillar, not sure if they had seen me or not. They were sitting at the gate directly across from mine waiting for the San Francisco flight to leave. I stood with my back to the pillar certain that any second my dad would stick his head around the corner and say something like, *"Small world!"* or *"Son, you're stuck between a rock and a hard place."* Then he and my mom would ground me for the rest of my life. But they must not have seen me because the only people staring at me were my fellow passengers. They probably thought I was a hijacker or something. In an attempt to look less threatening I slid down into a sitting position with the pillar against my back. I don't think it worked, but at least I was more comfortable.

I stayed in this position for at least ten minutes, then the most wonderful sentence I'd ever heard came over the loudspeaker: "Now boarding flight three-forty-three to San Francisco." I peeked around the pillar and saw my parents standing in line. They were holding hands.

After they got on their plane I almost left the airport and went home, but when they called my flight I found myself getting into line with the others as if I had no will of my own. When I decide I'm going to do something, no matter how stupid, I usually follow it through. My mom says that this is a terrible character flaw. My dad agrees with her except when it comes to sports, which I'm pretty good at. The flaw comes in handy when you're running a football down field, stealing a base, or trying to pin a wrestling opponent to the mat.

The flight to Bozeman was uneventful and I didn't

have any trouble getting to the hotel. When I checked in the clerk handed me two messages. The first was a reminder that the tour bus left for Mammoth Hot Springs in Yellowstone at 7AM the next morning. The second was a message from Theodore asking me to call him.

Up in my room I dialed Theodore's number, waited through ten rings, and was about to hang up when he came on the line.

"Just a sec," he said. In the background I heard printers rattling and the high-pitched whine of a computer modem connecting. After a couple of minutes he got back on the phone. "How was the flight?"

What makes you think I went? I thought.

"Fine," I answered. "Except I almost bumped into my parents at the airport."

"You're kidding?"

"They were at the gate right across from me."

"I should have thought of that."

"It's not your fault. I didn't tell you when their plane was leaving."

"Yeah, right," he said distractedly. "What did you tell your sister?"

"I told her I was going camping with a friend for the weekend."

"Perfect! It's even true."

Barely, I thought.

"What do you know about cults?" he asked.

"Nothing," I said. Although, on the plane I thought about what I would do if I happened to come across a cult in the woods. I didn't come up with much.

"I did some more checking on the Children Of Divine Light," he said. "It's not easy getting information on them. They're pretty secretive. But from what I've been able to gather they're raising a select group of children to take over the world or something. They believe that some catastrophic event is going to hit us sometime soon and they're training the kids as the earth's future leaders."

"What does this have to do with Amy O'Toole?" I asked.

"Her aunt is one of the founding members of C.O.D.L.," he said. "But I'm not sure if she's still a member. I'm having a hard time finding information on her which is pretty weird. Usually with a computer you can—"

"Wait a second, Theodore!" I interrupted. "I don't need a computer lecture right now. Are you saying that Amy's aunt has something to do with her disappearance?"

"Like I told you," he said. "It's a long shot. Amy's

mother, Sarah, has a twin sister named Bonnie."

"And you think she kidnapped, Amy?" He's gone off the deep end, I thought.

"I don't know if she nabbed Amy or not," he continued. "Sarah hasn't heard a word from Bonnie in over two years. Like a lot of twins they were close, then Bonnie dropped off the face of the earth. The police didn't think this was important."

And with good reason, I thought.

"How do you know Bonnie's even there?" I asked.

"I don't," he answered. "But I can't seem to find her anywhere else, so there's a good chance she's at the commune."

There was also a good chance that she had married and changed her last name, or moved out of the country, or didn't want to have anymore contact with her twin sister. This was what my dad would call a wild goose chase.

"Why am I here, Theodore?"

"Because we've got to cover all the bases."

Now Theodore was beginning to sound like my dad.

"If you find Amy," he continued. "Don't let on that you know who she is. Just take her photograph, then get out of there as fast as you can and give me a call. I'll take care of the rest."

"Right," I said. But as far as I was concerned the chances of finding Amy at a religious commune in the Montana wilderness were about a billion to one.

"Taking her photograph is very important. Without it, the police won't have any grounds for a search warrant. They've been trying to get in there for years, but so far they haven't come up with a reason that would hold up in court."

"I have a question," I said.

"Go ahead."

"Do I get paid ten dollars an hour when I'm sleeping?"

Theodore laughed. "Of course! You've been on the clock since you got to the airport. Oh, by the way, watch out for grizzlies. Someone was mauled in the park today. I saw it on the news."

"Great," I said. "Thanks for sharing that with me. I'll sleep a lot better now. Good bye, Theodore."

After I hung up I ordered a hamburger from room service, and turned on the television. "The Maltese Falcon" was on, based on the novel by Dashiell Hammett. Humphrey Bogart plays the tough private investigator, Sam Spade. I wondered how tough Spade would be if he had to face a grizzly.

9

Mammoth Hot Springs

The bus ride from Bozeman to Yellowstone took about two hours. The talk on the bus was all about the tourist who got mauled by the grizzly bear. Apparently he was walking in the woods, listening to a cassette player through earphones when he bumped into a female bear with a couple of cubs.

"That moron did three things wrong," the bus's grizzly expert said. "In the first place he was listening to that stupid cassette player. When you're hiking you've got to pay attention to what's going on around you. Second, instead of rolling up into a ball and staying put when the grizz attacked, he ran. Out runnin' a grizzly is like trying to outrun a horse."

I didn't blame the guy for running. I know I would have a hard time staying put with a seven hundred pound bear dripping saliva all over me.

"And third," the man continued. "The idiot left the

official trail and was wandering around where he shouldn't be. Grizzlies usually stay clear of trails that are regularly traveled by humans. If you use your head, grizzlies are harmless."

The guy in the hospital with two hundred fifty-three stitches probably didn't see it that way.

I looked at my map and checked the course Theodore had laid out for me. At the seven mile marker I was supposed to leave the official trail. Great! Ten bucks an hour didn't seem like enough money to be bear bait. But I'd gone this far so I figured I might as well complete the assignment. I only hoped my sister wouldn't have to tell my parents I had ran myself over with the lawnmower.

The bus pulled up in front of the hotel at Mammoth Hot Springs. The sign outside the hotel said the site used to be a cavalry outpost. In front of the hotel was a large expanse of manicured lawn. Wild elk roamed all over the place, bugling to each other, eating the grass, and ignoring the swarms of tourists with their clicking cameras. Next door to the hotel was a restaurant. I was starving, so I went inside to fatten myself up for the grizzlies.

When I finished eating I walked over to a little grocery store and bought enough junk food to last me a couple of days. I had no intention of living off the land like Paul Bunyan had taught us.

Outside the store there was a guy selling bear repellent. It came in a spray-can and he swore that it worked.

"If you get attacked just spray it in the bear's face. I guarantee he'll run away."

I hoped I never got that close to a bear's face, but I bought a can anyway. The can came in a small, canvas holder which I attached to one of the straps on my backpack.

So, I was set; food, camp gear, map, compass, and bear repellent. I found the trail head and started on my ten buck an hour hike into the wilderness.

It had been awhile since I'd been hiking with a full pack. The first couple of miles weren't too bad, but the next few miles were miserable. My pack felt like it weighed a thousand pounds. Other hikers with packs heavier than mine passed me as if I was standing still. In fact, the only things that weren't passing me were the mosquitoes. They seemed happy to swarm around my head as I slowly trudged up the trail. I finally got tired of swatting them and let them have my face and neck. And they probably would have sucked out my last drop of blood, but another hiker took pity on me and stopped. He sprayed me all over with bug repellent, which kept the mosquitoes away for about thirty seconds. I should have bought a can of bug repellent not bear repellent.

Finally, I reached the seven mile marker. I took my pack off and collapsed on the ground.

I wasn't very thrilled about the next part of the assignment. According to Theodore I was supposed to leave the trail here and head east for approximately three miles. He said it would take me out of the park and onto the land owned by the Children of Divine Light.

"All you have to do is wander around until you find their compound," he had said. "Or until someone finds you."

"You make it sound like I'll be in a park in the city," I told him. "Why can't I just take a cab up there? Or, walk up the road to their compound?"

"Because that's too easy."

"That's my point," I protested.

Theodore explained that the more effort I went through to get there, the better the chances were that the C.O.D.L. people would let me stay. It didn't make any sense to me at the time and it made less sense now.

What about the bears? What if I got lost? It wasn't like Theodore had actually been up here in a four-wheel-drive wheelchair. How did he know that the

Children Of Divine Light were three miles off the trail? Maybe they were ten miles away or twenty. Maybe their compound was to the north, not to the east. Another problem I had was that it had taken me a lot longer to get up the trail than I thought. It would be dark in a couple hours and I wasn't looking forward to spending the night with a bunch of cranky bears.

The way I saw it I had two choices. I could head back down the trail to Mammoth Hot Springs and forget the whole thing, but this would mean spending the night in the woods. My other choice was to leave the trail and try to find C.O.D.L. before the sun went down.

Neither choice was very good, but I decided to try to find C.O.D.L. because it seemed like my only chance for spending the night inside away from the bears.

Two hours and several miles later the sun started to set and the C.O.D.L. commune was nowhere in sight. I didn't know exactly where I was, and worse yet, no one else knew where I was either. I began to wish that Paul Bunyan was with me. He'd probably enjoy wrestling a bear.

I gathered wood and started a fire, hoping it would keep the bears away, not attract them. Once I had the fire roaring I wrapped myself in my sleeping bag and fell asleep sitting up with the bear repellent clutched tightly in my right hand.

A little while later something woke me up. I opened my eyes and looked at my watch. It was just after midnight. The fire was almost out and beyond it all I could see was darkness. I heard a loud cracking sound to my right. I tried to convince myself that it was just a deer, but somehow I knew it wasn't. I heard the sound again—this time closer. I put my index finger on the bear repellent nozzle hoping that it was pointed in the right direction, with my luck I'd spray my own face, not the bear's. Then I heard the voices.

"It was over here I tell you."

"I don't think so."

"Well, I'm going over this way."

"You think you guys are making enough racket? Pipe down for crying out loud."

Three flashlight beams crisscrossed along the ground about fifty yards away. Who were they? And why were they out in the middle of the woods at this time of night? Maybe they were hikers who had gotten lost and saw my fire. Whoever they were, they were headed right toward me and I was out in the open with no place to hide.

I thought about how Philip Marlowe would handle this situation. He'd be calm and try to talk his way out of it. "I'm over here," I called out. It seemed like the smartest thing I could do at the moment. I didn't want them to think that I was afraid, or that I had anything to hide.

The three beams bounced around in confusion for a few seconds, then found me. They walked over and shined the flashlights right in my face.

"What are you doing out here, kid?"

"How about getting the flashlights out of my face?" I asked.

"In a minute," one of them said. "You're on private property."

"Since when has Yellowstone National Park been private property?" I asked.

"You're not in the park anymore."

I thought about Philip Marlowe again. At this point he'd probably knock the flashlights out of their hands and slap them around a little. But this wasn't an old movie and I wasn't Philip Marlowe.

"I'm looking for the Children Of Divine Light," I said, standing up.

The three men stepped away from me and talked among themselves for a few seconds. I hoped I'd said the right thing. Theodore had mentioned that some of the locals weren't very happy about C.O.D.L. and there had been trouble in the past. The men came back.

"Why are you looking for them?" one of them asked.

"I want to join," I told him.

"You'd better come with us," he said.

"Where to?"

"We don't have all night kid," he said roughly. "Let's go!"

I didn't like the sound of his voice or his answer. I considered spraying them with bear repellent and running, but I didn't think I could outrun all of them. I turned around and slipped the repellent into the pack's side pocket where I could get to it quickly if I needed it.

One of the men led the way and the other two followed behind me as we walked to a Jeep Cherokee parked on a dirt road.

"Where are you taking me?" I asked.

Instead of answering, one of the men took my pack and threw it into the back of the Jeep. So much for reaching the bear repellent easily.

"Get in."

I stood there for a moment. "Not until you tell me where we're going."

"If you want to join C.O.D.L., you'll get in the Jeep."

"So you're from C.O.D.L.?"

"Just get in the damn Jeep!"

Not a very spiritual or enlightened response I thought, and climbed in the back. I guess I was earning my ten bucks an hour now.

10

The Children Of Divine Light

We drove a few miles down the road and came to a gate with a guard posted outside of it. He opened the gate and waved us through. We continued on until we came to a group of small log cabins and stopped.

"Let's go," one of the men snapped.

"Where to?" I asked.

Instead of answering he grabbed my arm and jerked me out of the Jeep. "Follow me," he said and the others laughed.

He dragged me onto the porch of one of the cabins, opened the door, pushed me inside, and slammed the door behind me.

"What about my pack!" I yelled, but no one answered.

The air in the pitch black cabin was stale, as if it had been closed for a long time. I tried to open the door, but it was locked. I felt along the walls for a light switch. No luck, but my hand did find a wood sliver the size of a toothpick. I also found a metal cot with my shin bone. The cot had a thin mattress with a musty smelling sleeping bag on top of it. The only good thing about the situation was that I was safe from grizzlies for the time being.

I sat on the cot trying to get the sliver out of my hand and cursed Theodore for getting me into this mess. He was probably asleep right now. Next door, my sister was partying with her goofy friends. My parents were in San Francisco enjoying their second honeymoon. And I was being held prisoner by a bunch of whackoes.

After I dug most of the sliver out, I laid down on the cot and covered myself with the damp, smelly sleeping bag.

Several hours later sunlight began to filter through the chinks in the logs and I was able to make out more of my surroundings. Not that there was much to see—the only thing in the cabin was the cot I was lying on.

A car pulled up outside and I heard the muffled sound of voices and footsteps on the front porch. I sat up just as the cabin door banged open. A man stood in the entrance. He had long, dark, greasy hair, and an ugly red scar that started on his temple and ended somewhere beneath his filthy shirt collar. He had a walkie-talkie clipped to his belt. Charming.

"Outside," he growled.

Good morning to you too, I thought as I stepped past him onto the porch. Across from the cabin, facing away from me, was a group of about twenty boys sitting cross-legged on the ground. Their heads were shaved and they wore long white robes with black belts tied around their waists. None of them could have been more than five years old, so I knew the black belts had nothing to do with the martial arts. They were being lectured to by a bald man dressed exactly like them, except he wore a light blue belt around his robe and he carried a long stick in his hand. I was too far away to hear what he was saying, but he was obviously teaching a class or something. A couple of kids turned and looked at me when I came out of the cabin. The man slapped the stick on the ground and their heads snapped back toward him like he had a wire attached to their noses. This really surprised me. I had three cousins about the same age and I couldn't have gotten their attention like that with a bucket of their favorite ice cream.

This had to be the C.O.D.L. commune, but it wasn't anything like I expected.

"Get in the car," Scarface snarled.

He didn't look like the kind of person who liked to debate things, so I got in the car without a word. He slipped behind the steering wheel and stepped on the gas. The car fishtailed, sending up a plume of dust, but not one of the kids turned to look as we drove away. What was the matter with them? And where were the girls? I wasn't going to find Amy in a boy's camp. Theodore and his fantasy case, I thought with disgust.

"Where are we going?" I asked.

"Sister Bonita," Scarface said without taking his eyes off the road.

"Who?"

Scarface looked at me like I was stupid. And who could blame him? I hadn't been acting like a genius over the past twenty-four hours. I should have been better prepared, but I didn't know how I could have anticipated this. Now what was I going to do?

One choice was to tell Sister Bonita the whole thing was a big mistake. That I hadn't meant to wander onto their property and if she would just give me my things back I'd be on my way. Ten bucks an hour was good money, but it wasn't enough for being locked in a stinking cabin and getting a wake up call from a guy who looked like he had spent the night in his own grave.

We passed several more log cabins tucked in among the trees. Outside a few of the cabins were small vegetable gardens, which were being tended by bald people wearing white robes. On the surface it seemed peaceful, but there was something going on here that wasn't right. Scarface and the three men who picked me up didn't fit into this tranquil setting.

"There's been a mistake," I said.

Scarface glanced at me.

"I thought I was in Yellowstone," I continued, thinking that I might as well try my story out on him before I tried it on Sister Bonita. "I didn't know that I was on C.O.D.L. land. If I can get my stuff back I'll just hike back to the park."

"Too late," Scarface mumbled.

That wasn't what I wanted to hear. "What do you mean?"

"Sister Bonita," he answered.

"I don't really want to take up her time," I told him. "She's probably pretty busy—"

"She wants to talk to you," he interrupted.

"It really isn't necessary."

"We're here."

We came around the corner and stopped in front of a large trailer. A man dressed in white came out and looked at me through the driver's window.

"This is him," Scarface said.

The man nodded and came over to my side and opened the door. "Please come with me," he said.

I didn't want to go, but he looked a lot more trustworthy then Scarface, so I got out. Scarface didn't waste any time. He turned the car around and headed back down the road.

The man looked me up and down, then shook his shaved head. I didn't like the way he was looking at me and wondered if I should have taken my chances in the car with Scarface.

"Follow me," he said.

I followed him inside.

"There's a shower in there." He pointed to a door.

"Shower?"

"Yes. Before you meet Sister Bonita, you must be clean. At least on the outside."

"I was just telling the other guy that there's been a mistake," I said. "If you could give me my stuff I'll just—"

"Too late," he interrupted. "You'll take a shower." He opened the door.

If taking a shower was the only way I could get my things back then I'd take one. I stepped into the room and he closed the door behind me. There was a changing room with benches and lockers, and through another door, three shower stalls. The sooner I get this over with the better, I thought. I took my clothes off and set them on the bench.

The shower felt better than I expected and I was comforted by the thought that they wouldn't ask me to take a shower if they were going to torture or kill me. When I finished, I dried myself off and walked back into the dressing room and saw that all my clothes were gone. In their place was a white robe, a bright red belt, and a pair of thongs still in their plastic wrapper. I picked the robe up, went over to the door, and stuck my head out.

"Excuse me," I said politely. "Someone seems to have taken my clothes."

"Yes," the man said, smiling.

"I don't really want to wear this," I said.

"You must."

I stared at him for a few moments, hoping the eye contact might change his mind. It didn't. I shut the door and pulled the robe over my head and tied the belt around my waist. There were no mirrors, but I didn't need one to know I looked pretty weird.

The man opened the backdoor of the trailer "This way," he said, then followed me outside.

Behind the trailer was a carefully groomed path. As we followed it I tried to think of ways to escape. I was pretty sure I could out run my guide, but then what? They had my return plane ticket, Theodore's money, and all my gear. I'd be stuck in the middle of nowhere dressed like a ghost. And the robe and thongs weren't exactly warm. When the sun went down I'd probably freeze to death.

"What do you wear during the winter?" I asked.

Instead of answering the man just smiled.

The path went uphill through a thick stand of trees. A narrow stream trickled next to it. It was actually a pretty spot. If I hadn't been wearing a goofy robe, escorted by Mr. Smiles, on my way to who knows where, I might have even enjoyed the walk.

We came to a large clearing. On the opposite side was the biggest log house I'd ever seen. It was surrounded by a log fence about ten feet high and at each corner was a turret manned by a white clad C.O.D.L. member. The three-story house in the middle of the compound was painted white and was at least half a block long. On the left end of the top floor was a large deck. On the other end, connected by an enclosed walkway, was another large log building with several skylights built into the roof.

When we got to the fence the man mumbled something into his walkie-talkie and the wrought iron gate leading to the compound swung open by remote control.

"This is where I leave you," the man said. "Sister Bonita is waiting for you in the cathedral." He pointed to the building with the skylights, then turned around and started walking back along the path.

I stood there for a few seconds debating whether I should walk into the compound or run away. If I went inside it might not be that easy to get out again. But why wouldn't they let me out? All I'd done was trespass a little. No big deal. I walked into the compound and the gate closed behind me.

11

Sister Bonita

A large stream flowed in front of the buildings. I walked across the footbridge to the door of the cathedral, and before I knocked, it swung open. I was greeted by two boys who were probably eight or nine years old. Like the other kids I'd seen, their heads were shaved and they were wearing the white C.O.D.L. uniform, but instead of black belts they had light brown belts around their waists.

"Your thongs," one of the boys said.

"What about them?"

"Take them off please."

I slipped the thongs off and the other boy picked them up and carried them away at arms length like I had stepped in something nasty. I thought about telling him they were brand new and that I'd only taken a couple of hundred steps in them, but I didn't think he'd listen.

The boy pointed. "Your feet."

"They don't come off," I said, trying to be funny, but the boy didn't crack a smile.

"I need to wash them," he said.

"You're kidding?"

He shook his head and pointed at a tiled wading pool built into the floor. I walked over to it.

"Please step in."

I shrugged my shoulders. It didn't look like it was filled with acid, so I did as he asked. The ankle deep water was warm and felt pretty good. The boy then proceeded to wash my feet with a soft brush. This felt pretty good too—although it was a little embarrassing.

When he finished, he dried my feet off with a towel and smiled up at me and said, "Thank you."

I looked down at him and thought, this is very weird.

He handed me another pair of thongs wrapped in plastic and I took them out and slipped them on.

"Don't you guys re-use these things?"

Instead of answering he said, "You may go in now." The boy who took my thongs held open a large door. I stepped through it.

Inside was a huge auditorium. Instead of chairs there were several hundred white cushions on the floor. At the far end of the room was a raised platform.

And sitting on the platform in a white chair was a bald C.O.D.L. member dressed in a white robe with a white belt tied around it.

"Please come forward, Peter."

Two things surprised me. First, it was a woman's voice. And second, she knew my name. It was like that scene in the Wizard of Oz when Dorothy and her gang meet the wizard in the Emerald Palace. "We're not in Kansas anymore, Toto," I thought and walked to the front of the auditorium.

"Please sit down," the woman in white said.

I sat on a cushion in front of the platform and looked up at her. For some reason she looked familiar.

"You must be Sister Bonita," I said.

"Yes."

"Well," I began. And I was about to explain to her that there'd been a big mistake, when a little kid with a shaved head ran across the stage and jumped into her lap. The kid giggled and pointed at me.

"He has hair!"

I tried very hard not to show my surprise. The little kid was Amy O'Toole. And I realized why the woman looked so familiar. Sister Bonita was Sara O'Toole's twin sister, Bonnie. She looked a lot different without hair.

"Amanda, you're not supposed to be in here," Bonita said crossly.

Amy's smile faded as if her aunt had slapped her. "Sorry, Mommy," she apologized and gave Bonita a slight bow.

"Amanda?" I thought. "Mommy?"

"Go back to your room and meditate," Bonita said, sternly. "I'll be in soon to see how you've done."

"Yes, Mommy," Amy said and bowed again. She looked like she was about ready to burst into tears, but she held them back. Tears probably weren't allowed. I wondered what four year olds thought about when they meditated.

Bonita watched Amy walk away, then turned back to me. "Sorry for that interruption, Peter. You were saying?"

I was too shocked to say anything now. Amy thought Bonita was her mother and didn't even know she had been kidnapped. Seeing Amy also meant that Theodore wasn't insane. If anyone was having a fantasy it was me, not Theodore. His long shot had led directly to the solution.

"Are you all right, Peter?" Bonita asked.

"Sure, I'm fine." I said, but I wasn't. Seeing Amy had changed everything.

"You look strange," she said suspiciously.

"Just tired," I said quickly. "And hungry."

"Of course," she said, relaxing a little bit. "Why are you here?"

"I want to join the Children Of Divine Light," I answered, surprising myself.

"I see," she said calmly. "Before we discuss that, I have a few questions for you."

"All right."

"We're an open community," she began. "As such, what belongs to one of us belongs to all. So, we took the liberty of going through your pack."

So that's how she knew who I was. My name and address were on the name tag. Luckily I had left all the information about Amy in my bedroom back home.... Then I remembered the photograph of Amy. I'd left it in my shirt pocket and they had my shirt. Philip Marlowe would not have made this mistake. My stomach felt queasy and I thought for a moment that I might throw up.

"You walked in from Mammoth Hot Springs?" she asked.

"Right."

"I see," she said. "We noticed your airline ticket says that you are returning on Monday night. If you wanted to join the Children of Divine Light, then why were

you planning to leave on Monday?"

"I didn't know if you'd let me join," I lied.

She nodded. Here it comes, I thought. *We also found the photograph of Amy and now we're going to kill you.* I held my breath.

"I'm sorry you had to spend the night in the cabin," she continued. "We're very careful about trespassers. We have many enemies."

I let my breath out. "Well, I'm not one of them."

She didn't say anything.

"What about my clothes?" I asked casually.

"I beg your pardon?"

"When I was taking my shower someone took my clothes."

She smiled. "You'll get them back. I imagine they've been taken to the laundry. We don't allow those kind of clothes in the compound. Don't worry about it."

Easy thing to say, I thought. It was only a matter of time before they discovered the photo and turned it over to her. I had to get away from there before they found it.

"So you want to become a member of our community?"

"Well, I'm not sure," I stammered. "You see—"

"I'm afraid you can't join us," she interrupted. "In

the first place you're a minor. We don't allow minors here without their parents."

Unless you've kidnapped them, I thought.

"And the children we have here are much younger. We've found that it's too late for children over the age of five years."

"Too late for what?"

"Too late to learn the way," she answered.

"What's the way?"

She smiled pleasantly. "I'm afraid you'll never know."

"Well, that's too bad," I said, trying to look very disappointed. "It looks like I came all the way out here for nothing."

"I'm sorry," she said. "We'll have someone drive you into Mammoth Hot Springs later tonight. Or, if you prefer, we'll take you to Bozeman. Perhaps you can catch an earlier flight."

"Tonight?" I wanted to leave immediately.

"Yes," she said. "We won't have anyone available until later this evening."

"I don't really need a ride. If you'll just give me my things back I can hike out of here right now. I don't want to be a bother." And I didn't want to be there when they found the photo either.

"I'm afraid that won't be possible," she said. "We

76

want to make sure you get back safely. If something was to happen to you and they found out you had been here, we might get in trouble. You understand of course."

I nodded, knowing more about her troubles than she could imagine.

"So what time will I be able to leave?"

"I'm not sure. We only have a few cars up here. It won't be until late, after our evening service. In the meantime, we'll give you something to eat and a room you can rest in. You must be tired after last night."

"I am."

"If you want to see the rest of the commune later, I'll assign you an escort. He'll be able to get you some food as well."

"Thanks," I said, without much enthusiasm. I had to figure a way to get out of there. "Maybe I should call my parents and let them know what's going on."

"That's an excellent idea." She reached behind her chair and came up with a cordless phone and handed it to me. I was hoping for a little more privacy, but I could see she wasn't going to give it to me. I dialed anyway.

When Theodore answered I said, "Hi, Mom!"

"What?" Theodore asked.

"I'm at the commune."

"Pete?"

"That's right."

"Are they on the line?"

"Heck no."

"But they're listening to you?"

"Right."

"Is Amy there?"

"Sure is."

"That's fantastic!" he shouted. "What a lucky break. Did you take her photograph?"

"Nope, and I won't be able too either."

"Why not?" he asked, obviously disappointed.

"Give me a break," I said cheerfully.

"Oh, right," he said. "I guess you can't go into a lot of detail right now."

"Not at the moment."

"Do they know why you're there?" he asked.

"No, but they will pretty soon."

"That's bad. If they find out they'll move Amy and we'll probably never find her again."

Yeah, I thought. And what about me, Theodore? Thanks for asking.

"I'll contact the authorities," Theodore continued. "But even if I convince them that Amy's there, they probably won't be able to get into the compound before she's been moved. It could take them days to get a search warrant."

"Oh, well," I said smiling.

"I guess you'll just have to get her out yourself."

"You've got to be kidding," I said, trying to keep the fake smile plastered on my face.

"It's our only choice."

"Ours?" I thought. You're not here, Theodore!

I glanced at Bonita, or Bonnie, or whatever her name was. "Okay," I said into the phone. "I'll be home Sunday night. They're going to drive me to Mammoth Hot Springs this evening. Okay, Mom. Love you too. I'll see you then. Bye."

I hung up the phone. "No problem," I said to Bonita, relieved that she hadn't grabbed it from me and discovered that my mom was an adolescent boy in a wheelchair.

"Well good," she said. "I'll introduce you to your escort. He'll take you to your room. After you rest he can show you around if you like." She leaned forward and put her hand on my shoulder. "I'm sorry this didn't work out, Peter. Perhaps one day you can bring your own children here and they can learn the way."

Or maybe I'll bring them to visit you in prison, I thought. And they can learn what happens to an aunt who kidnaps her little niece.

12

Brother Thomas

The guy that Bonita assigned to me was a guard, not an escort. Like the other guards he had a radio hanging from his belt.

"My name is Brother Thomas," he said. "I'm here to serve you."

Yeah, I thought—like a tennis ball if I get out of line.

Brother Thomas was probably thirty years old and had arms bigger around than my waist and absolutely no neck. I figured they must have a weight room somewhere, because muscles like his didn't come naturally. Even Paul Bunyan would have been impressed.

He led me upstairs to my room.

"If you need anything just ask," he said.

"I think I'll take a nap."

"Sister Bonita said you were hungry."

"Maybe later."

"Fine. I'll be right outside." He closed the door to

the room.

The first thing I did was check the window to see if I could use it as an exit. Negative. I was on the top floor facing the front of the house and in clear view of at least two of the guard towers. If the fall didn't kill me I wouldn't get very far before someone grabbed me. A couple windows over was the balcony I'd seen from below. If I was careful I might be able to reach it, but then what? I'd still be on the top floor and with my luck the room it led to would probably be filled with people dressed like ghosts.

My room had a bed, a night stand, and a lamp—that was it. Nothing that was going to help me escape. Across from the bed were two doors. Behind the first door was a bathroom. I walked in and checked the medicine cabinet above the sink. All I found was a bottle of aspirin, a bar of soap, a package of disposable razors, and a can of shaving cream. Not much help.

I walked back into the main room and opened the other door. It was a small closet and hanging inside were half a dozen white robes and several different colored belts. I reached for the belts thinking I might be able to tie them together and lower myself from the window after it got dark. Then I noticed something underneath the robes.

My backpack! I yanked it out and tore it open hoping to find the shirt I'd been wearing with a wash-ruined photo in the pocket. No shirt, no photo, no luck. The camera was also missing, which meant that even if I saw Amy again I wouldn't be able to take her photograph. Everything else was there including the can of bear repellent. I grabbed the bear spray, then sat on the edge of the bed and thought about my options.

It was only a matter of time before they found the photograph of Amy. When they did, I was certain things were going to get very bad for me.

I decided that the first thing I needed to do was to get out of the stupid robe. I took it off and put on my spare jeans, shirt, and tennis shoes. Having my own clothes on made me feel better. I left my shirt tail out and stuffed the bear repellent into my waistband, then looked in the bathroom mirror to make sure no one could see it.

As promised, Brother Thomas was waiting for me outside in the hallway.

"What's this?" he asked, pointing at me.

I thought he'd seen the bear repellent and I was about to whip it out from under my shirt and spray him with it when he added, "I suppose the clothes will be all right since you're leaving soon."

"I felt a little uncomfortable in the robe because I'm not an official member," I said quickly.

He nodded. "I thought you were going to rest?"

"I guess I wasn't tired. I'd like to get something to eat. Then, if you have time, maybe you could show me around."

"I'd be happy to," he said, but I could tell he wasn't thrilled about it. He led me downstairs to the kitchen and asked the cook to give me some food. The cook explained that they were all vegetarians and proved it by serving me a bowl of soup and a sandwich without a gram of animal fat or meat. My sister Teri would have loved the food, but I don't think she would have liked being bald.

After I finished choking down the bland food, Thomas took me outside and started showing me around. The first place we went was the C.O.D.L. garage where Sister Bonita had three white Rolls Royces. When I asked Thomas why she needed three identical cars he explained that they had been gifts and she couldn't sell any of them without insulting one of the donors.

"She told me that the reason she couldn't take me to

Mammoth was because no cars were available," I said.

Brother Thomas smiled. "The only person who can ride in these cars besides Sister Bonita and Sister Amanda is their driver."

"Amanda?"

"Sister Bonita's daughter."

"Oh, yeah," I said. "I met her."

He looked surprised. "What a great honor," he said, solemnly.

I shrugged my shoulders. "How long has Am... Amanda been here?"

"She's always been here," Thomas said.

Now it was my turn to look surprised. "You mean you saw her here when she was a baby?"

"No one laid eyes on her as an infant," he said. "Sister Bonita kept her isolated."

"Why?"

"Because it was prophesied that the *Chosen One* would not be looked upon until her fourth year."

How convenient, I thought. "Chosen for what?" I asked.

"To lead the Children of Divine Light after the great calamity."

"Isn't Sister Bonita the leader?"

"Of course. But when she passes on she'll be succeeded by her blood daughter, Sister Amanda."

"And what's this great calamity supposed to be?"

Instead of answering he smiled mysteriously. I figured he didn't have an answer to this and I was tempted to give him my theories on the subject, which had to do with Bonita getting busted for kidnapping.

"Would you like to see our airport?" he asked, changing the subject.

"Airport?"

"Come."

We walked across the yard to the entrance. Brother Thomas mumbled something into his radio and the gate swung open.

"Do you always keep this gate locked?" I asked.

"Yes. Except during the evening services."

I filed that away for later use and followed him along a wooded trail to another large clearing. In the middle of it was a long, paved runway. He took me into the hanger and showed me C.O.D.L.'s white Lear jet and a helicopter, which he said was used for patrolling their property.

I had wondered how they had gotten Amy out of town without anyone seeing her. Now I knew. They simply flew her here in the private jet and probably snuck her into the cabin at night so no one would see her.

Airports keep records of when planes come and go.

If we could prove that Bonita's jet took off from the airport on the day Amy disappeared it might be enough to nail her. If I figured a way out of here, that might be something I could use.

13

The Grand Tour

Over the next several hours I learned more about the Children of Divine Light than I really wanted to know.

Thomas told me that the colored belts represented different levels of enlightenment—black being the lowest rank and white being the highest. Apparently, Bonita interviewed each member every few months and decided what color belt they could wear. Thomas wore a light blue belt, so I figured that in addition to being a guard, he was also one of the higher ranking priests.

"What about the guys who picked me up?" I asked. "They weren't wearing robes."

"They're C.O.D.L. employees," he explained. "We need a certain number of support staff to help us deal with the outside world."

"Why did you choose Montana?"

"The location was revealed to Sister Bonita in a divine revelation. She was told to come here and train a few chosen followers and their children as priests."

He went on to explain that C.O.D.L. had thousands of followers all over the world, but only the most devout were invited to enter the priesthood. And if you wanted to become a priest it was also helpful if you had a child under the age of five that could be trained. I figured that's why Bonita had kidnapped Amy. She didn't have a kid of her own and she wanted a successor who was related to her.

As far as I could tell, all you had to do to become a non-priest member of C.O.D.L. was to give them a lot of money. This bought you a place on what Brother Thomas called, *The Sacred Scroll.*

"What sacred scroll?" I asked.

"I'll show you." He led me to an area outside the compound that was surrounded by a chain-link fence. Inside, buried in the ground, was a huge concrete building half the size of a football field

"This is our shelter," he said, proudly. "When the calamity comes only those on The Sacred Scroll will be allowed to enter. There are five underground levels and we have enough supplies to last us for years."

"How many C.O.D.L. priests are there?" I asked.

"We have two hundred in residence here, but there are a thousand priests worldwide."

"You mean there are other camps?"

"We have a half dozen camps in different countries. This is the only camp in the United States."

"And Sister Bonita is in charge of all of them?"

He nodded and looked up at the sky. "It's getting dark. We should probably get back. Our evening service will be starting soon."

The whole time Thomas was showing me around I was looking for an opportunity to spray him with bear repellent and run away, but I never got the chance. Wherever we went there were people around. And the later it got the more people there seemed to be.

We left the shelter and followed a path to the main house. The priests were beginning to gather outside the fence, sitting in groups divided by belt color. The kids sat towards the back, and standing in front of each group of kids, was an adult carrying a stick.

"What's with the sticks?" I asked, as we made our way through the crowd.

"Those are correction rods," he stated simply.

"You mean you hit the kids with them?"

"No, we *correct* them. Spare the rod, spoil the child is our philosophy. There is much for the children to learn and we have very little time until the end. Discipline is absolutely necessary."

Now I understood why the kids had acted the way they did when their leader had banged the stick on the ground, and why Amy obeyed Bonita so quickly when her aunt got angry with her. The kids were terrified. *Correcting* the children with sticks was wrong. If they beat the kids with sticks, what would they do to me if they found the photograph?

As we stood in front of the gate the priests raised their hands and looked toward the house. They began chanting. I followed their gaze and saw Bonita and Amy standing on the balcony looking down at the crowd.

"What's going on?"

"We're preparing for our service," Thomas said.

Before I knew what was happening the gate opened and he ushered me through the entrance. As soon as we were inside two priests ran over to us and took Brother Thomas to the side to talk to him. I knew something was wrong. I turned and looked at the gate, but it had already swung shut.

When I turned back, the three men were staring at me and they didn't look very happy.

Thomas was holding a photograph in his right hand.

14

Locked Up

They hurried me into the house and up to my room. I thought about using the bear repellent, but if I was lucky enough to get all three of them, where would I go? There were a couple hundred people in front of the house, to say nothing of the guards in the towers.

Thomas shoved me onto the bed. "Where did you get this photograph?"

I didn't answer him. I needed time to think.

"Where did you get the photo of Sister Amanda?" he repeated.

"I don't know what you're talking about."

"It was in your shirt pocket," Thomas said. "No one is allowed to have photos of the Chosen One."

"Well, I don't know how it got in my shirt pocket. I didn't put it there. I've never seen it before!"

"The only way he could have gotten the photo was to steal it from Sister Amanda's living quarters," one of

91

the other men said.

"How could that be?" I protested. "I haven't been alone since I got here!"

All three men stared at me. They didn't seem to have an answer for this.

"And in the photograph, Amanda has hair," I added. "How do you explain that?"

The two men with Brother Thomas looked confused. And for a moment I thought I might be able to convince them that Amy wasn't Sister Bonita's daughter.

Thomas smiled. "The explanation is simple," he said calmly. "Sister Bonita took the chosen one's hair only recently."

The two men nodded as if that was the most reasonable answer in the world. So much for convincing them that Amanda was Bonita's niece, not her daughter.

Thomas walked over to the window and looked out. "The service is about ready to start," he said, turning to the other two men.

"What should we do?" one of them asked Thomas.

"Does Sister Bonita know about the photo?"

The men shook their heads.

"In that case, it will have to wait. I'll talk to her after the service. She'll know what to do."

He was right, I thought. Bonita would know *exactly*

what to do. As soon as she saw the photo she would probably have me killed.

"We'll leave him in the room," Thomas said. "I want one of you to stand watch outside his door."

They started to leave.

"Hey, wait a second!" I yelled.

Brother Thomas paused and looked at me. "It will be over soon," he said, closing the door behind him.

I didn't like his parting words and I had a feeling that he knew Amy wasn't Bonita's daughter. When I had asked him earlier if he'd seen Amy when she was a baby, he hadn't really answered me. Bonita must have had help kidnapping Amy and it made sense that Thomas and others close to Bonita knew about it.

I looked out the window. It was almost dark now and the priests were filing through the open gate. The children's groups had split up and each kid was holding hands with an adult as they walked into the auditorium.

I got my bear repellent out and walked over to the door. I took hold of the knob. On the count of three, I told myself. One, two, three... I jerked on the knob and almost tore my arm out of it's socket—the door was locked.

"Stay away from the door!" the guard shouted from the other side.

So much for Plan A, I thought and went over to the

window to take a look at Plan B.

Outside, the gate was closed and everyone was in the auditorium except for the guards in the towers. I quietly opened the window and looked down at the ground. It was about a thirty foot drop. If I climbed out the window and dangled by my arms I could probably cut the fall by six feet, but that wouldn't be enough to prevent me from breaking every bone in my body when I landed.

I went to the closet and grabbed the C.O.D.L. belts hanging above the pack. There were four belts and when I tied them together I had a makeshift rope about seven feet long. If I tied it near the window I'd knock off another six feet and have a decent chance of hitting the ground without killing myself.

Unfortunately there wasn't anyplace to tie the rope! I spent fifteen frantic minutes trying to figure out how to solve this dilemma, but it was no use. It wasn't going to work.

Plan C. I didn't have a Plan C!

I sat on the edge of the bed in the dark, breathing deeply, trying to calm myself down and stop thinking about what was going to happen when the service was over...

I'd hear footsteps coming down the hall. The door would

open and Brother Thomas and the other two thugs in white
would come in and kill me. They'd take my body into the
wilderness and dump it off a cliff so it looked like an acci-
dent. Bonita and Amy would take off in the Lear jet.

It would be that simple. The police would investigate, and they might even figure out what really happened and catch them, but what good would that do me?

I went back over to the window and looked down. Considering the alternative of certain death, the drop didn't look as bad as it had a few minutes earlier. But there was one slight detail I hadn't considered. If I got lucky and landed without breaking anything, how would I get out of the compound?

A white robe, I thought. Of course! After I made the jump all I'd have to do is to hide until the service was over, then walk out through the gate with the other priests. By the time Brother Thomas discovered I was gone I would be well on my way to Mammoth Hot Springs.

I grabbed a robe out of the closet, took it into the bathroom, and pulled it over my clothes. When I looked in the mirror I noticed a slight problem with the plan. My hair.

I'm not vain and I don't spend a lot of time looking in mirrors, but one thing that I like about myself is my hair. There had to be a way of getting out of the compound without shaving it off, but I couldn't think of one, and time was running out.

I wet my hair down and sprayed a pile of shaving cream on top of my head and rubbed the foam into my hair. That was the easy part. I held the disposable razor with a shaky hand for a long time before I gathered enough courage to make the first swipe down the center of my scalp. The result was horrifying and I had to stifle a loud moan so the guard outside the door wouldn't hear me.

Grimly, one sickening swipe at a time, I scraped the rest off. When I finally finished I wanted to weep. I managed to nick myself several times and had to stick bits of toilet paper on the cuts to stop them from bleeding. Theodore was going to have to do a lot better than a computer for this sacrifice.

I didn't want Brother Thomas to know I'd shaved my head so I cleaned the hair out of the sink and flushed it down the toilet, then straightened up the bathroom as best as I could.

I went into the other room and dug my map, compass, and flashlight out of my backpack, and stuffed them into my hip pocket. The backpack and all the other gear was going to have to stay behind. There was no way to get it out of the compound without giving myself away. I was ready, or as ready as I could get under the circumstances. I walked over to the open window and leaned out, looking for what I hoped would be a soft landing spot.

"What are you doing?" someone whispered.

The voice startled me so badly that I stood straight up and cracked the back of my bald head on the edge of the open window.

I heard a giggle.

"You're funny," the voice whispered.

I looked over to my right and saw Amy staring at me through the slats of the balcony rail.

Plan C

Why wasn't she at the service with her mother?

"Come over and play with me," she whispered.

"No," I whispered back. "Quiet!"

"If you don't come over here. I'll come to your room." She started to leave.

"No! Wait!"

All I needed was for her to skip down the hall and tell the guy outside my door that I had invited her over to play.

She stopped. "Are you going to come over then?" she asked.

I thought about it for a second. The balcony must lead to Bonita's living quarters where there was probably a phone. I could call for help. The only reason I hadn't considered the balcony in the first place was because I thought there might be people in the room. If there wasn't a phone I could always tie the belts to the bottom of the balcony rail.

"Are you alone?" I asked.

She nodded. "Mommy's downstairs talking."

"And no one else is with you?"

"Nope."

"All right Amy, I'll come over. But you'll have to give me a few minutes. Okay?"

"Okay."

"Stay right where you are."

"Okay, I promise."

"Good."

I popped back inside and wrapped the belts around my waist. I hoped Amy was telling the truth about being alone. Now all I had to do was to get to the balcony without falling to my death.

I stuck my head back out the window, relieved to see Amy still sitting there.

"Hi," she whispered.

"I'm going to climb over to you," I whispered back.

"Why don't you use the door?"

"It's more fun this way."

There were two windows between me and the balcony, and thirty feet of air between me and the ground. Some fun, I thought.

"You could fall!" Amy whispered.

"I won't," I said confidently, trying to stop my legs from shaking.

I climbed outside and stood on the narrow sill and gripped the top of the window frame above my head. This is stupid, I thought, and started inching my way toward the balcony. It wasn't bad until I got to the end of the first sill. To get to the next window I had to stretch across a five foot gap. This maneuver was further complicated by the fact that I couldn't see what I was doing because I had to hug the wall and my robe kept snagging on the rough logs. But I made it. The next window wasn't any easier, but I managed to get to it without falling. Now all I had to do was get across to the balcony.

Unfortunately, the gap between me and the edge of the balcony was at least ten feet across and there was no way I could stretch that far. I wanted to cry. It looked like there wasn't any choice but to go back the way I'd come and take my chances dropping from my window. But how would I stop Amy from running down the hallway and telling the guard?

I turned my head to talk to her and saw that she was gone! I cursed, thinking that she was probably already blabbing to the guard, then I heard a tapping sound. I looked left and right, but couldn't figure out where it

100

was coming from. The tapping came again, only this time it was accompanied by a muffled voice.

"In here!"

It was Amy. She was standing in the window I was clinging to, waving her hand. I almost fell over backwards. In the process of regaining my balance my flashlight slipped out of my pocket and fell to the ground—so much for light. I motioned for her to open the window. She dragged a chair over and flipped the latch. I helped her get the window up and climbed through.

"Hi," she said shyly.

"Hi." I looked around the dark room.

"This is my mommy's room," she whispered. "We're not supposed to be in here."

"We'll leave soon," I told her. "Does your mommy have a phone in here?"

"She takes it with her."

I remembered the cordless phone Bonita had with her earlier in the day. "There must be another phone."

"Yep," Amy confirmed, nodding her head.

"Great! Show me were it is."

I followed her into the next room. There was a wood stove in the corner and several chairs and sofas strewn about.

"So, where's the phone?" I asked.

"Here!" she exclaimed, holding up a walkie-talkie.

Perfect, I thought. I can use it to call the C.O.D.L. guards and tell them I'm about to escape. "Is there another phone?" I asked hopefully.

Amy shook her head.

So much for that option. I took the radio from her anyway and put it in my back pocket under the robe. I could always throw it away if I didn't find a way to use it later.

"What time does your mommy finish talking?"

She giggled and pointed to my new hairdo. "You got paper on your head."

I brushed the bits of toilet paper from my scalp. "So what time does she finish?"

"Why do you have so many belts?" she asked.

"Amy, I need to know what time your mom gets up here so we won't get in trouble."

"My name is Amanda now."

"Fine," I said, impatiently. I didn't have time for this. "When will your mom get here?"

"Soon."

That's what I was afraid of. I went out onto the balcony and began unwinding the belts from around my waist. Amy followed me.

"I have to go," I said.

"Why?" she asked loudly.

"Shhhhh! You've got to be quiet or we're going to get in trouble."

"You said you'd play with me," she said and started to cry.

All I needed was her to throw a tantrum on the balcony and attract the guards in the towers. I took her hand and led her back inside.

"Amy, this is serious. If I don't get out of here I won't be able to come back and play with you ever. Do you understand?"

She nodded, but the tears kept rolling down her little cheeks. "I don't have anyone to play with."

"I know," I said, wondering what Bonita would do with her once she figured out people on the outside knew she was here. Theodore thought Bonita would take her away and hide her, but what if he was wrong? Cults sometimes did strange things. The newspaper was full of mass suicide packs, murders, and other horror stories. What if something happened to Amy because I'd shown up at C.O.D.L.? How would I feel?

Not good, I concluded. Not good at all. And I knew then that I was going to have to figure out a way to take her with me. That's what Philip Marlowe would do. I guess it was time for me to start acting like a real operative.

I told Amy to stay on the sofa and I walked out to the balcony. The chances of making it to the ground without one of us getting hurt were zero. There had to be another way.

I walked back inside and sat down next to her. She had stopped crying, but she was still very unhappy. I not only had to find a way out of there, I also had to talk or trick her into coming with me willingly.

"Your daddy's waiting for you," I said.

"My daddy's dead," she said, sadly.

"No he's not," I insisted. "I just talked to him. He's waiting for us in the woods."

She shook her head. "Mommy said he died."

"Well, she was wrong. Because he's waiting for us in the woods."

"Are you lying?" she asked.

"Nope. He wants us to go to him."

"I have to ask Mommy."

"There's no time," I insisted. "We have to leave now or he'll go away again."

"Mommy will be mad if I don't tell her first. She'll hit me!" she said, glancing at the wall near the wood stove.

A correction rod was leaning against the wall. I

walked over and broke it over my knee.

"Your daddy doesn't want you to be hit ever again," I said, stuffing it into the wood stove. "No more corrections!"

I couldn't tell if Amy was going to cry or laugh, but breaking and burning the stick sure got her attention.

"You'll have to do everything I say," I told her.

"I don't know," she said, still wavering.

Time was running out. My new plan was to sneak downstairs and hide outside until the priests started to leave. I was hoping that we'd be able to join them without being noticed. For this to work though, I needed Amy's help.

I rubbed my scalp, desperately trying to think of something to say that would convince her that it was all right. Then it came to me.

"Your daddy has your hair," I said.

"He does?"

"Yep. But he's going to throw it away if you don't go see him."

"I want my hair."

"Then you better come with me."

"I better ask Mommy."

"There's no time!" I said. "We've got to go now or you'll never have hair again."

"I want my hair back!" she said with certainty.

I had her!

"Okay, Amy. If you want your hair back, then you'll have to do exactly what I tell you to do."

"I promise," she agreed.

"Good. The first thing I want you to do is show me your room."

She led me into a small room that was furnished like the room they had put me in. In other words it didn't look at all like a little girl's room. There were no pictures on the wall, no toys—just the bare necessities. I opened the closet and found the clothes Amy had been wearing when she was kidnapped.

"I want you to put these on," I said.

"Mommy says I can't wear outside clothes anymore."

"Just put them on, okay?"

She pulled her robe over her head and I helped her put on the jeans, red tee-shirt, tennis shoes, and pink coat. I slipped her robe over the top of the clothes and tied a black belt around her waist.

"I wear a white belt," she said. "Like Mommy."

"Not anymore. You've been demoted."

The white belt would be like a neon sign around her waist. For this to work she had to look like all the other little kids. And she did, except for a little lumpiness

106

caused by the clothes under the robe. I hoped that in the dark no one would notice.

We walked back into the other room and I took out the bear repellent and put it up my sleeve. I wanted it handy just in case the next part of my plan didn't work.

"What's that?" Amy asked.

"Bear spray."

"For when I get my hair back," she said, happily.

Cute kid. "Exactly," I said.

I opened the closet door near the front door and looked inside. It was perfect. All I needed now was a way to lock it. I found a wooden chair in the living room that might do the trick.

"Okay, Amy," I said. "We're going to play a game."

"Good! I like games."

"What I want you to do is to open the front door and tell the man in the hallway that there's something bad in the closet. Then I want you to run to your room as fast as you can and hide under your bed."

"Okay," she said, eagerly.

I hid behind the closet door and told her to go ahead.

She opened the front door and shouted, "There's something in the closet! It's bad!"

Amy ran to her bedroom and I heard the guard hurry down the hallway. When he got inside he walked right into the closet. I slammed the door shut and jammed the back of the chair underneath the doorknob. After I was sure it was secure I ran into Amy's room and got her from under her bed.

"What's that noise?" she asked.

The guard was trying to beat the door down.

"Ghosts," I answered, taking her hand.

16

Escape From The Wicked Castle

We made it downstairs without any problems. As we walked by the hallway leading to the auditorium we heard music playing and people chanting. It sounded like the service was in full swing and I hoped it would stay that way until we found a place to hide outside.

I opened the front door and pulled Amy through quickly, closing the door behind us. We hurried over to the small stand of trees near the foot bridge and squatted down in a place where I hoped we couldn't be seen from the house or the guard towers.

My plan was to wait for the priests to start filing past, then simply stand up and walk out of the compound with them. I figured that it would take awhile for Brother Thomas to explain the situation to Bonita. Then she would have to figure out what she wanted to do about it. By the time they discovered we were gone, Amy and I would be well on our way.

I realized there were a couple of major flaws in my plan. The fact that it was dark was both good and bad. It would be hard for them to find us in the dark, but it would also be hard for us to get around. Another glitch was that I didn't exactly know how to get back to Mammoth Hot Springs. I had an idea of the general direction, and I had my map and compass, but I wouldn't be able to use the map in the dark. The other problem was Amy. She was going to slow us down considerably and I had no idea how long it would take for her to get tired of the whole thing and tell me that she wanted to go back home.

"We're going to play another game," I whispered.

"I like games," she whispered back.

"Good. It's called, Escape from the Wicked Castle. In order to play we need to follow the ghosts through the castle gate. But to make it to the woods safely we have to fool the ghosts into thinking that we're ghosts too."

"How?" Amy asked.

"By not talking."

"Why?"

"Because these ghosts don't talk, and if we talk they'll know we're not ghosts."

"What happens if they catch us?"

"They'll take us back to the castle and eat us."

"I don't want to be eaten," she said.

"Me either. So we'll both have to keep our mouths closed."

She nodded and I asked her to tell me the rules again.

"We don't talk so the ghosts think we're ghosts so they don't eat us," she said. "And when we get to the woods I become a princess."

"Exactly," I said, smiling at her new ending.

The front door to the auditorium swung open and the priests began to file out. Several of them flicked on flashlights. They walked in complete silence, their lights casting strange shadows across the compound. I was half convinced that they were ghosts. Settle down, Pete, I told myself.

"Okay," I whispered, nervously. "Here come the ghosts, not a word from now on."

The priests started across the compound towards the foot bridge. The wrought iron gate opened and I had to will myself not to jump up and run through it ahead of them. Our only hope of getting out of the compound un-noticed was to fall in behind the last priest in line.

It seemed to take them forever to make their way

111

across the foot bridge. As we waited I imagined Bonita holding the photo in her hand. She was probably feeling the same panic I was experiencing hiding behind this tree. In a matter of minutes Brother Thomas would discover we were gone and the search would begin.

Finally the last of the priests started over the bridge. Amy and I left our hiding place and quietly fell in behind them. One of the priests glanced back at us, but he didn't seem concerned that we were there and continued walking. With each step toward the gate I expected to hear shouts of alarm behind us, but nothing happened. We simply walked through the gate with the other priests. When we were through, the gate closed.

We followed the group down the path for awhile, then I pulled Amy off into the woods.

"We win," she whispered.

"Not yet," I said. "We still need to be quiet."

I pulled her robe over her head and saw that her coat was going to be a problem. The pink seemed to glow in the dark. I checked the coat's lining and was thankful to see that it was dark blue. I unzipped it.

"It's cold," she complained.

"I know," I said, taking her coat off. "We need to change the color of your coat so the ghosts don't see you."

I turned the coat inside out, then helped her back

into it.

"They won't see you now," I said, taking off my robe and dropping it next to Amy's. "As soon as we bury these ghost costumes we can go."

"And find my daddy," Amy said.

"That's right."

"And my hair."

"Exactly."

She helped me cover the robes with dirt and leaves. I glanced at the house and saw the light in my room go on. They would start searching the house now and it wouldn't take them long to discover that we weren't inside.

The chase was on.

17

The Dragon

As soon as we started walking through the woods I knew my initial plan wasn't going to work. Amy was just too small to step over the fallen branches without stumbling. I picked her up and headed toward the main road. She was heavier than she looked. When we reached the road, where she couldn't trip over anything, I set her down and we started walking again.

"Where's my daddy?" she asked.

"A little further into the woods," I told her.

"How long before we see him?"

"Pretty soon."

By now they knew we weren't in the house. The way I figured it, Bonita would either get in her Lear jet and leave the country, or she would come after Amy. I'd know soon which choice she had made.

"Now what are we going to play?" Amy asked.

I had to think about this for a minute. "We're going

to play, Escape from the Dragon," I said. "It's kind of like Hide and Seek. Have you ever played that?"

"Sure," Amy said. "But how do we know if the dragon's coming?"

"By looking for the light of his fire," I told her. "Every time we see a light we need to hide in the forest. If the light touches us we'll catch fire."

"But it's not for real," Amy said.

Just as she said this, headlights appeared from behind us.

"Yes it is," I said.

I grabbed her and jumped off the road. We were near one of the cabins. The windows were dark and I thought about hiding inside, but decided not to. Instead, I carried Amy to the woodpile outside the cabin and hid behind it.

The car stopped on the road and a man got out with a flashlight. He was bald like a C.O.D.L. priest, but instead of a white robe he was wearing regular clothes. He must have seen us, I thought, taking the bear repellent out of the holster. But instead of looking around, he walked straight down the path leading to the cabin and knocked on the door. The lights went on inside and the door opened. I couldn't believe that I'd thought about hiding in there.

"Were you asleep?" the man with the flashlight asked.

"Just about. What's up?"

"I'm not sure. Apparently someone's missing or lost or something. Brother Thomas wants us to meet him at the cathedral. They're setting up search parties and Sister Bonita wants to talk to us."

"Who's missing?"

"Don't know. But he said for us to put on outside clothes. Sounds like a long night."

"Sure does. Come on in while I change."

The man with the flashlight stepped inside and a couple minutes later they both came out and walked back to the car parked on the road.

"Amy you were great!" I said, and I meant it. The whole time they were talking I was afraid she was going to move or say something, but she hadn't.

"Those weren't dragons," she said. "Those were priests."

"But they work for the dragon," I said, picking her up.

From their conversation it was pretty clear that Bonita wasn't going anywhere until she found Amy. I'd have to stay off the roads and stick to the woods even if it meant carrying Amy the whole way. At least I was in pretty good shape from football practice. I felt like a halfback on a thousand mile playing field and

Amy was a thirty pound football. How was I going to avoid all the C.O.D.L. linemen, and more importantly, which direction was the goal?

A couple hours later I stopped to rest in a little clearing near the edge of what looked like a steep ravine. My back and arms ached from carrying Amy, but we had covered a lot of ground and hadn't run into one person, which I was very happy about. I wasn't exactly sure where we were and I wished the sunrise would hurry up so I could look at the map. The only thing we had to guide us was my compass with the luminous dial. Mammoth Hot Springs was somewhere to the east of us.

"I'm tired," Amy whined. "I want to go home."

So do I, I thought. The only thing that surprised me about her complaining was that she hadn't done it sooner. She was a great kid and very trusting. It must have been a cinch for Bonita to snatch her. This was something Amy's parents were going to have to work on with her. Providing I got her back to them.

"I want to go home," she repeated.

"What about the dragon?"

"There's no such thing as dragons," she said. "That's

just a game. Take me home."

"What about your hair?" I asked.

"I don't want my hair."

"What about your daddy?"

"My daddy's dead."

So we were back to that. I didn't know if I had the energy to start it all over again, but I had to try.

"Amy, your daddy—"

I heard a loud noise and suddenly a helicopter appeared out of nowhere with its giant search light sweeping across the clearing. It stopped right over the top of us, blowing grass and sticks all over the place.

"The dragon!" Amy screamed.

I scooped her off the ground and started running toward a stand of trees. I was sure they had seen us and I knew the other C.O.D.L. members wouldn't be far behind.

"We'll burn up," Amy yelled. "I don't want to burn up."

I wanted to comfort her, but there wasn't any time. I was running full speed and the helicopter was right behind us. As soon as we got into the stand I hid behind a tree. The helicopter swooped over trying to spot us with its searchlight. By now it had radioed the others and they would move in for a ground search.

Amy was crying hysterically now. "I want to go home," she moaned.

"I'll get you home, Amy. I promise," I shouted above the noise. "But first we have to get away from the dragon."

When the helicopter flew passed us I moved deeper into the woods right behind it. When it swung back around I hid behind a tree and waited to move forward until it passed over us again.

After about a half hour of this helicopter hopscotch, it started to make wider swings and I was convinced that it hadn't spotted us since we ran into the woods. The wide swings it was making allowed us to move further and further away. After a couple hours we were at least three miles from the search area, but I knew this wasn't far enough. We had to keep moving.

I carried Amy up and down hills and across small streams. I had no idea where we were, but the dragon was gone and we were safe. At least for now.

When my arms got tired I put Amy on my shoulders, when my shoulders started to ache I transferred her back to my arms. After awhile she fell asleep and didn't even wake up when I moved her.

We came to the edge of what looked like a huge meadow and I knew I couldn't go any further. I was cold, tired, and hungry. I collapsed on the ground next to a fallen tree. There was just enough room underneath it for us to hide and get some rest.

As I closed my eyes I thought about Theodore. He was our only chance of being found by the authorities. I hoped that he was awake, trying to get us out of this.

18

The Three Bears

"Doggies!" Amy shouted gleefully.

At first I thought I was dreaming. I opened my eyes and saw the tree trunk overhead. The sun was just coming up. I was pretty groggy and it took awhile for me to remember where I was.

"Doggies!" Amy repeated.

What was she talking about? I crawled out from under the log and saw her standing up, pointing across the meadow.

"See?" she said.

I looked. The meadow was covered with a light ground fog. In the middle of it were two grizzly bear cubs. One of them was standing on two feet sniffing the air, looking in our direction.

"Those aren't doggies!" I shouted, starting towards her.

Just as I was about to grab her, I saw four men come

out of the woods on the far side of the meadow. None of them had hair. The second cub stood up and snorted in alarm.

"There they are!" one of the men shouted.

I swept Amy into my arms and started to run. I'd only taken a couple of steps when I heard a very loud bellowing sound. I glanced back, and stopped when I saw what was happening.

There were now three bears standing in the center of the meadow—two little bears and one giant mother bear. She wasn't very happy about the four bald men standing a hundred feet away from her cubs. The men weren't very happy either.

The mother grizzly charged them and I was shocked at how quickly she moved. But not as shocked as the men were. They turned and ran for their lives back towards the woods.

"Bad doggies," Amy said, watching the men run.

"No way!" I shouted. "Good offensive lineman!" It was nice to know that I wasn't alone on the playing field.

"I'm hungry," she said. "I want to go home now."

"We'll be there soon," I told her and we started off again.

If the bear didn't catch them, I knew the search party

would regroup. It wouldn't be long until they were after us again. I walked through the woods for a couple of miles, then stopped to rest.

"I want my mommy," Amy said.

"I know. We'll find her." But I didn't believe it. Despite the bear running interference for us, it was only a matter of time until they found us.

"We could call her," she said."

"We don't have a phone."

"In your pocket."

I pulled the radio out of my back pocket. "This isn't a phone, Amy."

"Mommy talks on it."

"I know, but it's not a real phone. See, there are no numbers on it."

I handed it to her and she turned the knob on top.

"Did you copy that?" a man asked.

"Negative."

"See," Amy said.

I grabbed it away from her and turned up the volume. I thought I might get lucky and hear the grizzly bear tearing those guys apart.

"We're near Arrowhead Meadow," the man continued. *"We had them, but we got chased off by a bear."*

"I copy that. What direction were they heading? Over."

"I'd guess they're about a half a mile from the trail by now. We're not far behind them."

"Roger. Continue pursuit."

I put the radio back in my pocket, then took out my map and found Arrowhead Meadow. They had just told me where we were! I spread the map out on the ground, and with my compass, plotted a course to the trail.

"We've got to go, Amy." I picked her up and started jogging.

It didn't take long to find the trail. About half an hour later we came across a sign with the most beautiful words I'd ever seen: Mammoth Hot Springs - 2 miles. I set Amy on the ground, let out a whoop of joy, and jumped in the air.

Amy stared at me and I think she was a little frightened by my outburst.

"Do you know what that sign says?" I asked.

She shook her head.

"It says home, Amy."

She grinned. I picked her up and started down the trail to Mammoth Hot Springs.

19

The Goal Line

I set Amy on the ground and caught my breath.

"Is Mommy here?" she asked.

"Not exactly," I said. "But we can call her from that building."

We were at the trail head. The only sounds were the distant calls of elk bugling to each other. All I had to do was get Amy into the lobby of the Mammoth Hotel. There were people with hair in there—people who would help us. To reach the hotel we had to cross an open space of about two hundred yards.

"Let's call Mommy," Amy said. "And eat."

I picked her up and started across the lawn. To my surprise, no defensive tackles ran out after us and no cars burnt rubber trying to block our way. It was just a quiet morning at Mammoth Hot Springs and I was a bald tourist carrying a little girl in my arms. The playing field was wide open, but about halfway across the lawn all this changed.

"Men," Amy said. "Running."

At first I didn't know what she was talking about. All I saw was the Mammoth Hotel drawing nearer. Then I realized that she was looking over my shoulder back at the trail head. I turned around. Brother Thomas and Scarface were sprinting across the lawn toward us. Thomas looked a lot different with street clothes, but there was no mistaking his muscle-bound body.

I put Amy down. "Run!" I shouted. "Go to the building! Your mommy's inside waiting for you."

But it was too late. Amy didn't take more than three or four steps before the men were on us. Scarface scooped Amy off the lawn like a hungry hawk snatching a mouse. An instant later, Thomas slammed into me like a meteorite and drove me into the ground. Before I could regain my breath he grabbed my arm and yanked me to my feet.

"Time to go," he said with an evil grin on his face.

Amy was struggling to get out of Scarface's arms, but it was futile. I looked over at the hotel just in time to see a white Rolls Royce pull up in front. The rear door opened and Sister Bonita stepped out, but she didn't look like a priestess anymore. She was wearing regular clothes and had a wig on. She looked exactly like the photo of Amy's mother I had seen.

"Mommy!" Amy shouted, struggling harder to get out of Scarface's clutches.

Just then, a helicopter appeared from behind the trees and started moving toward the lawn.

"Amanda!" Sister Bonita yelled. "Come to—" Her words were drowned out by noise of the helicopter rotors.

"The Dragon!" Amy shouted in terror.

With my free hand I reached for the bear spray clipped to my belt and shot a stream into Thomas's face. He dropped to the ground like I'd hit him with a flame-thrower and started choking and gagging. Scarface put Amy down and ran toward me. I pushed the nozzle again and he joined Brother Thomas writhing on the ground. Two down, one high priestess to go. I ran after Amy.

I caught her before she reached Bonita and picked her up. "That's not your mommy, Amy."

"Yes it is!" she insisted.

Three police cars came roaring down the road with their sirens blaring and lights flashing. At that same moment, the helicopter landed and a man and a woman jumped out of it before the rotors stopped whirling.

"Let me go," Amy screamed. "I want to go to my mommy."

"I'll take you to her." I turned away from Bonita and started toward the helicopter.

"Mommy's by the car!" Amy insisted.

"No, Amy. Your Mommy's by the dragon and your Daddy's with her. Look!"

Amy's parents sprinted across the lawn. I didn't know how they had gotten on that helicopter and I didn't care. I was just happy to see them, but not half as happy as Amy's parents were to see their daughter. With tears streaming down their faces, they took Amy from my arms and hugged her with joyful relief.

"You've been busy," someone said from behind me. I turned around. It was Uncle Willy, dressed in a three-piece suit, carrying his ivory-headed cane. He was with another man. "This is Lieutenant Boswell, from the Montana State Police."

"What happened to your head?" the Lieutenant asked.

"It's a long story."

"I'm sorry it took us so long to get here," Uncle Willy continued. "We thought you were still at the C.O.D.L. commune. When we didn't find you there we flew back hoping you'd show up here. Looks like we got here just in time."

"Were you flying around last night?" I asked.

"No," he said. "We flew out of Bozeman early this

morning."

"Well, I'm glad to hear that," I said. At least I hadn't ran from the good guys the previous evening. They both looked confused and I explained about the encounter with the C.O.D.L. dragon the night before.

I looked across the lawn at the white Rolls Royce. Bonita was flanked by two policemen. She was looking at Amy and her parents hugging each other. I'm sure the site didn't make her very happy.

Brother Thomas and Scarface were still on the ground gagging. A group of policemen were helping them by snapping handcuffs on their wrists. After they were cuffed, the police hauled them to their feet.

They didn't look so good. Their eyes were red and swollen. Tears ran down their faces, but they weren't tears of joy over the happy reunion.

Amy's mother came over and threw her arms around me. "We'll never be able to thank you enough, Pete."

"No problem," I said.

Uncle Willy grinned.

20

Youth Sleuths

It took several hours to get everything straightened out. The police took statements from everyone. Bonita, Brother Thomas, and Scarface were arrested and taken away.

When it was all over we discovered that the helicopter wouldn't hold five passengers for the flight back to Bozeman. Uncle Willy told Amy's parents they could take the chopper and we'd rent a car and drive to the airport in Bozeman.

On the way, he told me that the case was over for me and I probably wouldn't have to appear in court.

"It's best to keep you and Theodore out of it," he said. "Your parents might be upset if they knew."

That was an understatement! I was going to have enough trouble explaining my bald head to them. I decided to tell them that Stanley and I made a bet and I lost. They were going to be mad, but knowing Stanley like they did, they wouldn't doubt the story for a minute.

I leaned against the window, closed my eyes, and didn't wake up until we got to the airport.

On the airplane I asked Uncle Willy how he and Theodore had become partners. He got a sad, far away look in his eyes.

"It was late at night," he began. "I'd been out drinking with the cast of *One Day to Remember*—"

"You mean the soap opera?" I asked.

"Yes," he said. "I played William Sampson on the show for fifteen years."

No wonder he liked to watch the soaps, I thought.

"Anyway," he continued. "I was driving home one evening, thinking about the next day's shoot, when Theodore ran out from behind a parked car. I didn't see him, but I probably would have if I hadn't been drinking. I hit him—severed his spine and ran into another car. The only injury I got was a bum leg, poor little Theodore never took another step."

"I had no idea."

"Theodore doesn't like to talk about it much," he said. "I went to the hospital everyday to visit him. I took a leave of absence from the show, joined Alcoholics Anonymous, and got off the bottle."

131

"But who started the YS Detective Agency?" I asked.

"Theodore," Uncle Willy said. "During our conversations at the hospital he told me that he wanted to be a private detective when he grew up. The agency started out as a game, really. Something to keep Theodore's mind off things, but Theodore took it very seriously. We started to get cases and Theodore solved them without ever leaving his house. I did the leg work and he did the brain work. He has a real genius for it."

I couldn't argue that with him. "And you never went back to the soaps?"

He shook his head.

"Do you miss acting?"

"Not at all. Oh, I like to watch the soaps on television, but I've found that real life is a lot more interesting."

I sat there awhile, letting all this sink in. "What does the YS stand for?" I asked.

"Youth Sleuths," he said, chuckling. "It was something we came up with in the hospital. We're both a little embarrassed about it now, but I don't think we'll change it."

"And do his parents know about this?"

"They certainly know about me," Willy said. "We've become pretty good friends since the accident. But they don't know about Theodore's real part in the detective agency. They think it's something I allow Theodore to help me with, when in reality I'm the one helping him. They're just happy that Theodore has something to occupy his time."

"Amy's parents are happy too," I said.

Uncle Willy smiled. "Indeed they are. Thanks to you."

We didn't get home until late that evening. Uncle Willy dropped me off at my house.

The front door was locked and I didn't want to wake up my sister so I went around to the back porch. I opened the screen door, switched on the light, and before I knew what was happening, my dog Spike was trying to kill me. I fell backwards down the stairs. Spike bit my leg, and when I tried to push him off, he bit my hand.

"It's me, Spike!" I yelled. "It's me!"

He stopped snapping at me, but continued to growl. Until that moment, I had no idea that he hated bald people.

I stood up and heard the back door open.

"Pete?" Teri asked nervously.

"Yeah, it's me," I said in disgust.

"What's going on out there?" She demanded.

"Spike and I are just playing," I said, stepping into

the light.

"What happened to you?" she yelled, staring at my head.

"I lost a bet with Stanley." I started up the stairs. Spike continued to growl behind me.

"You look stupid," Teri said. "Mom and Dad are going to kill you."

I brushed past her and turned on the kitchen light. It was a disaster area. I walked into the living room. It looked worse than the kitchen.

"I think you're the one who's going to be killed," I told her.

"I had a little party," she said. "I'll get it cleaned up tomorrow and you're going to help me."

I laughed. "What makes you think that?"

"If you don't," she shrieked. "I'll tell Mom and Dad that you shaved your head."

I just stared at her. "I think they'll figure that out on their own. Don't you?"

I walked upstairs to my room before she could respond. I barely got my clothes off before I dropped on the bed and fell asleep.

21

No Glory

I didn't wake up until late the next morning. I went into the bathroom and took a shower, trying very hard not to look at myself in the mirror.

The only thing I found in the kitchen to eat was some stale cereal. Everything else had been devoured by my sister's friends. There was no milk and no clean bowl to put it in. I ate a couple handfuls out of the box.

Before I went out the backdoor I put on my baseball cap so Spike wouldn't rip my throat out. He growled a couple of times and eyed me suspiciously, but settled down after he heard my voice.

I threw the ball for him a few times hoping to re-establish our relationship. As soon as his tongue was dragging on the ground I walked over to Theodore's house.

Theodore was outside on the patio. It was a cool morning and he had a wool blanket over his lap with a newspaper resting on top of it.

"Congratulations," he said, casually.

"Thanks," I said simply, not wanting to be 'out-casualed' by him.

"We'll have a check for you tomorrow and I guess I owe you a computer."

During the last twenty-four hours I'd been too busy to think about the money and now I was too tired.

"I lost all your gear. And the cash you gave me."

"No big deal. The reward will more than cover it."

I was happy to hear that.

Theodore handed me the local newspaper. On page three there was a photo of Amy and her parents at the airport with a headline that read: *Local Detective Agency Finds Missing Amy.*

I read the short article beneath the photo and was disappointed that Theodore's and my name hadn't been mentioned once.

"Uncle Willy made sure they didn't put your name in there," Theodore explained, reading my mind. "Being a public hero isn't everything it's cracked up to be. To be a good Op you have to be invisible. No glory, I'm afraid."

I didn't like it, but I knew it was for the best. My parents would have been pretty upset. "How did Uncle Willy arrange that?" I asked.

"He told the cops you were a runaway and he was going to take you back home. Considering all you did to get Amy out, he asked them to keep your name out of it. He convinced them you were already in enough trouble as it was."

"But what about the statement I made to the police?" I asked.

"They'll bury it," Theodore said. "They won't need it. The two guys you doused with bear juice spilled their guts about Bonnie kidnapping Amy."

"What will happen to Bonnie and the others?"

"Jail," Theodore said. "But it's going to be done very quietly. The C.O.D.L. board of directors apparently didn't know anything about Amy's kidnapping. They actually thought she was Bonnie's daughter and they want to minimize the bad publicity. And Amy's parents just want to get on with their lives. So in a few days it will be like it never happened."

Maybe for you, I thought. I wouldn't be forgetting it anytime soon.

"So, your parents come in at three today," Theodore said, changing the subject.

"That's right," I said. "But how do you know?"

Theodore smiled. "Who do you think made the plane reservations?" he asked.

"You what?" I shouted.

"How else was I supposed to get them out of the way? I hope they had a good time."

"I'm sure they did, Theodore, but—"

"By the way," he interrupted. "We have another case." He took a folder out from under the blanket. "It has some interesting aspects that—"

"Wait a second, Theodore!" I said, throwing my hat on the ground in frustration. "I could have been killed during this last escapade."

Theodore stared at me with his mouth open. At first I didn't know what he was looking at, then I realized he hadn't seen my new hairdo. He was obviously shocked at the sight.

"Look," I said. "I give people about two days to get used to the fact that I don't have any hair glued to my head. You're embarrassed, but it doesn't embarrass me."

Theodore started laughing so hard he dropped the folder on the ground. I joined him. When we finally finished I picked the folder up, but I didn't give it back to him right away. I had to see what was inside.

Amy's Missing

by
Roland Smith

Send me _____ copies of **Amy's Missing at $4.99 each.** I am enclosing $_____ (please add $2.00 to cover shipping and handling). Send check or money order — no cash or C.O.D.s please. YS Press, P.O. Box 1611, Wilsonville, Oregon 97070

Name _____

Address _____

City _____ State/Zip _____

Phone (_____) _____

Please allow four to six weeks for delivery. Offer good in the U.S. only.
